To,

MW01126016

Thank you for
Choosing Life

Constance Witt
7/5/18

The Legacy

ONE CHANCE, ONE CHOICE, FOR ONE LIFE

CONSTANCE WRIGHT

WESTBOW
PRESS®
A DIVISION OF THOMAS NELSON
& ZONDERVAN

WestBow Press books may be ordered through booksellers or by contacting:

WestBow Press
A Division of Thomas Nelson & Zondervan
1663 Liberty Drive
Bloomington, IN 47403
www.westbowpress.com
1 (866) 928-1240

Because of the dynamic nature of the Internet, any web addresses or
links contained in this book may have changed since publication and
may no longer be valid. The views expressed in this work are solely those
of the author and do not necessarily reflect the views of the publisher,
and the publisher hereby disclaims any responsibility for them.

Any people depicted in stock imagery provided by Thinkstock are
models, and such images are being used for illustrative purposes only.
Certain stock imagery © Thinkstock.

ISBN: 978-1-5127-1777-8 (sc)
ISBN: 978-1-5127-1778-5 (e)

Library of Congress Control Number: 2015917655

Print information available on the last page.

WestBow Press rev. date: 11/15/2016

In loving memory of my parents,
Willie and Juanita Wright

Chapter One

Annah stood in front of the nurse's station slowly rubbing her hands together, her palms moist from sweat and her eyes fixed on Christina. She watched as, one by one, members of the Lee family took each other's hands and filled the small luminous cardiac ICU room on the fourth floor of New York University Hospital. Their emotions ran quiet, but their pain was evident in the flow of tears. Annah ran her fingers slowly through her short brown curls and let out a deep sigh. *"What happened?"* she murmured under her breath. She reflected on the events leading up to the code blue on Christina. Her mind carefully reviewed each step she and the team of three doctors and four nurses took during the six-and-a-half-hour surgery. From the prep work down to the intricate details of the surgical thread she used for closing, everything had gone according to plan, thought Annah. Nothing could have been more accurate. Except, her patient was dead.

Annah looked on as Christina's mother, Ming, leaned over and adjusted the hospital blankets up to Christina's neck, carefully covering the long incision on her chest almost as if she were tucking her daughter in bed for the night. Ming kissed her daughter's face and said a few words in Mandarin, then she gently removed the surgical cap from Christina's head, allowing her daughter's long, jet-black hair to cascade down her shoulders. Mr. Lee stood on the other side of the bed stroking his daughter's face with one hand, and with the other he attempted to catch his tears before they fell on her cheek. Christina's skin still belied her lifelessness. Something in Annah wanted to deny her own reasoning, to believe her patient had merely slipped into a coma so deep it evaded traceable vital signs. But she knew better. Annah remembered the precise moment she had to pronounce Christina. She stumbled over her words before she managed to verbalize the time of death. In disbelief, she pulled off the surgical gloves, dropped them on the floor, and left the intensive care room to begin a deliberative analysis of what had taken place. The moment would remain with her forever—the first time she lost a patient, an 11-year-old child.

The orderly wheeled the crash cart out of the room, and the two nurses who assisted in Annah's failed attempt to resuscitate Christina joined the family to comfort them. Annah knew she did not have long before she would need to make the agonizing trek from the nurse's station to confront the family as to why Christina died. She struggled to find words of comfort, but nothing came to mind. Now she was forced to recite the speech she memorized as a first-year intern. *That's the problem with being a prideful perfectionist*, Annah thought. You don't prepare for the inevitable. She procrastinated as long as she could. The sweat continued to pour into the palms of her hands. She took in several deep breaths and exhaled. Her emotional discomfort zone now beckoned her appearance. She wiped the sweat from her hands on her white doctor's coat and practiced the speech in her head, ensuring she had the appropriate tones and inflections in her voice. But even in her mind she had to admit the "We did everything we could do, but I'm sorry your loved one didn't make it" speech sounded contrived. In just seconds, Annah relived the surgery again, from start to finish. She tried in vain to convince herself to just let it go. But she couldn't. Her mind taunted her with the conversation she'd had with Christina's parents a week prior to the surgery in which she assured them that performing the procedure would increase Christina's life expectancy. *I've performed this procedure over 100 times. Why did it fail me this time? What went wrong?* Annah thought about 71-year-old Mr. Winchester's recent quadruple-bypass surgery she performed two weeks prior. He was discharged from the hospital saying he felt like he could live another 30 years. So why would a child who was strong, die? Annah had no answers, and that in and of itself was not good enough for her to accept. She needed answers. Not for Christina's parents, but for herself. She wasn't comfortable with the emotions associated with failure.

"Excuse me, Dr. Kentwell? The family is ready to see you," said Irene, the head nurse, between sniffles, and a handful of tissues held to her nose.

"I'm ready." Annah sighed, running her fingers back through her hair. "So, how are they? Christina's parents?"

"It's not at all what I had expected," said Irene as she blew her nose and tried to fight back tears.

"What were you expecting?" Annah asked.

"I don't know. But if I'd just lost my only child I would be hysterical. These two seem pretty calm."

"Everyone reacts to death differently."

"I just wish everyone would react the same as Christina's family. It would make our jobs a whole lot easier."

Annah was relieved to have Irene as one of the team of nurses who cared for Christina, and she appreciated her ability to connect with patients. Empathy and warmth seemed to ooze from Irene's pores when she interacted with critically ill patients and their families, and she never seemed to mind serving as Annah's buffer. It was the perfect tag team. Annah performed the surgery on the patient and passed the ball to Irene to nurture matters of the soul.

Annah paused before she entered Christina's room. Her palms now coated in sweat, she placed her hands inside the pockets of her doctor's coat. She scanned the faces of the parents, grandparents, and a woman who had been introduced as Christina's aunt. Annah stood at the foot of the bed, her eyes glued to Christina. She cleared her throat.

"Mr. and Mrs. Lee, I am so very sorry for your loss," she said in an almost monotone voice. "We did everything we possibly could do to save your daughter's life. I can only assure you there were no complications during the procedure, and we have no explanation for her going into full cardiac arrest an hour after her surgery. If you have any questions for me, I can address them at this time." Annah expected to be bombarded with questions, but the only thing resonating was the continuous sound of sobbing from the family members. Christina's mother stepped forward and took Annah's hand in hers, exposing her wet palms.

"Christina was the joy of our lives." Her voice trembled. "We never once regretted conceiving a child in our forties, and we have no regrets for making the decision to move forward with the surgery. Our family is grateful to you and everyone here at the hospital for taking such good care of our little girl."

"Dr. Kentwell, do you have any children?" asked Christina's grandmother while tenderly massaging Christina's hand.

Annah hesitated. "No, I do not," she responded, unable to look her in the eye.

"When you do, then you will understand it's not just Christina we will miss. We will also miss not knowing who she was to become."

"Our family is at peace because Christina is at peace. The choice for her to enter life and leave us now is not in our hands," said Christina's father, Mr. Lee, touching Annah's forearm. Annah's discomfort heightened. She withdrew her hands from Mrs. Lee and stepped back to buffer their close proximity. She wanted nothing more than to leave the room.

"You are welcome to remain here with Christina as long as you need," Annah managed to blurt out. "If you have any more questions, any one of our nurses can page me." Relieved that the family had no further questions, Annah's mind leapt to the next logical step in what would help to settle the barrage of her own questions concerning Christina's death: an autopsy.

"Dr. Kentwell, are these the family members of your patient?" asked Dr. Rivas as he entered the ICU room, halting Annah's abrupt departure.

"Yes, Dr. Rivas," Annah said. She expected him to come, but not so quickly. In his 20 years as chief of staff at New York University Hospital, Dr. Rivas had made it his personal policy to meet with the family members of any patient who died on his watch and offer his condolences.

"I'm so very sorry for your loss," Dr. Rivas said to the Lee family. "I want you to know you could not have asked for a finer cardiologist to perform the surgery on Christina than Dr. Kentwell."

"Thank you, Dr. Rivas. I know Dr. Kentwell is a woman who carries a great wealth of knowledge, and she has carried it since childhood," Mr. Lee said, staring at Annah. He bowed slightly and turned back to Christina, but his words pierced Annah's heart. *It's just a coincidence,* she thought. *It's impossible for him to know about me. I've been too careful.*

"Dr. Kentwell? May I please see you for a moment?" said Dr. Rivas.

"How can I help you?" Annah said as they left the room.

"I've called a special meeting at 9:00 a.m. tomorrow in the executive boardroom, and your presence is requested."

"Is there anything I need to bring in preparation for this meeting?"

"No."

"May I ask what is the purpose for this meeting?"

"Just be there," Dr. Rivas said, walking away.

Probably a meeting with the Mortality and Morbidity Review Board, Annah immediately assumed. She wondered how Dr. Rivas had managed to assemble the review board so quickly. She thought it unlikely for him to presume that Christina had not made it through surgery, but given the rarity of quadruple-bypass surgery performed on a small child he may have thought otherwise. She had never before come before the Mortality and Morbidity Review Board. The board had a track record for intimidating even the most stubborn and pretentious doctors. Despite her discomfort in connecting with her patients, Annah had a love affair with practicing medicine. She felt alive walking the halls of the hospital, and with such state-of-the-art equipment and committed doctors at her disposal, Annah felt almost invincible in treating Christina's rare heart condition.

The Lee family remained in the room comforting one another, occasionally stroking Christina's hair and kissing her face, and finally joining hands together in prayer. Annah was intrigued by their ability to display affection. She quickly banished any thoughts she had about her own family. The only memory she allowed herself to revisit was the day 25 years ago she boarded a Greyhound bus in Ashton, Nebraska with a one-way ticket in her hand, headed to Yale University.

Anxious to prepare for what she anticipated was tomorrow's review board meeting, Annah quickened her steps down the intensive care corridor to the elevator. Before the doors opened, she turned to take one last look at Christina's room. She felt no connection to her patients, no connection to her colleagues with whom she worked, no connection even to her own family. She had a successful career as a doctor, but privately her life was empty. Annah stepped into the elevator, and as the doors closed she captured one fleeting thought. Perhaps she was the one who was dead, not Christina.

Chapter Two

Annah eased open her right eye and peered at the alarm clock on her nightstand--it read 6:20 a.m. She faintly remembered dozing off somewhere around 2:15. Her body ached. She sat up slowly on the side of the bed and took in deep breaths, hoping to eliminate the unsettling feeling in her stomach. Standing, she felt dizzy and lightheaded, and forced her body back down to the bed. It had been over a week since she first felt this way. "Ignore it. It's not what you think it is," she whispered. But the nausea would not relent, and not being in control was difficult for Annah to accept. This time, she had no choice but to give in. She took in another deep breath, released it, and rolled over to face the window. The nausea subsided. It was perfect timing. The rising sun peered through the sheer white curtains that framed her bay window, just like it did when she was a child in her bedroom back in Ashton. It was the very reason why Annah bought this Manhattan condo--it connected her to the single memory of childhood that she savored. Within minutes, the previous night's coolness was put to rest by the sun's rays, warming her room and making her feel as if she were being hugged from the inside out.

Annah gathered her strength and got into the shower, allowing her body to be brought fully awake by the cold water. She was physically fatigued, but her mind raced with thoughts of the morning's Mortality and Morbidity Review Board meeting. She was amply prepared for her inquisition, and felt confident in her ability to answer any questions the board had concerning Christina's case. *Irony,* she thought. The hospital board she once faced to gain permission to conduct the procedure on Christina would be the same board that would serve as her judge and jury in Christina's death. The warm water running through her hair and down her back seemed to rinse away any lingering doubts that she'd made the right decision to perform the surgery.

Annah walked into the first-floor boardroom at 8:45 a.m., relieved to find no one had yet arrived. The large cherry wood conference table and mahogany chairs scented the room. Antique frames lined the gold-patterned wallpaper holding pictures of former chiefs of staff, board members, and philanthropists. It was the very room where Annah's career at New York University Hospital began. In an intense three-and-a-half-hour interview, she convinced all nine board members that she was ready, at age 22, to begin her internship. She hoped this time she could manage to be just as confident. Annah traced her fingertips around the stack of medical records she'd placed on the table, each folder bearing the word "Deceased." It was surreal and unfair, Annah thought. Three months of testing her patient, grueling hours of research, hundreds of hours spent with a team of doctors she personally selected, only for her patient to die, and with no apparent evidence to support her death. Annah eased her body into the welcoming leather chair and closed her eyes. *Just let it go,* she said, attempting to console herself. *Just let it go.*

"Dr. Kentwell?" Dr. Rivas's upbeat voice caught Annah off guard.

"Dr. Rivas. Good morning," Annah said, standing.

"Please, Dr. Kentwell, be seated."

Annah sat across from Dr. Rivas, striving to assume the same posture she did 18 years ago at her interview, completely self-assured and impervious.

"Dr. Kentwell, you are one of the finest doctors in this hospital, and we are very proud of your accomplishments. You are not only knowledgeable in your field, you are not afraid to think outside the box. I've watched you over the years perform surgeries with perfection. And in your fifteen years as a cardiac surgeon, you have had one loss, your patient Christina. I find your almost zero fatality rate not only remarkable, but it also says a lot about you and your standard of excellence." Dr. Rivas sat back in his chair and peered at Annah over his bifocals.

She could picture Dr. Rivas in his younger, slimmer years. He was probably a handsome man prior to the typical weight gain around his midsection and receding hairline. Interns were either intimated by his 6'4" stature or avoided him altogether for his uncanny ability to expose a person's true motives. Annah respected Dr. Rivas chiefly for his diplomacy. No matter the circumstances, he had a distinct ability to maintain balance between being a gentle lamb and a roaring lion.

"I took the liberty of doing some background research on your work and your career."

"I'm sorry," Annah interrupted. "What does this have to do with my patient's death yesterday? And I was expecting the other members of the board to be here. I've spent hours going over Christina's records and…"

"Dr. Kentwell," Dr. Rivas interrupted, his hand on Christina's medical records, "this meeting has nothing to do with your patient."

"Then what is this about?" Annah said, raising her eyebrows.

"I want to personally inform you of mine and the board's decision."

"And what decision is that?"

"Your promotion to chief cardiac surgeon."

"What? Chief cardiac… I don't know what to say."

"Then just say yes."

"Well, yes. I'm honored, of course. I knew Dr. Sawyer was leaving in six months, but I had no idea the board was looking to fill the position so soon."

"Dr. Sawyer decided he wanted to start transitioning the new chief in the next month or two so he could take an even earlier retirement."

"I had no idea I was even being considered."

"Dr. Kentwell, you are the best I have seen in decades. You have proven yourself as an outstanding surgeon, and you have displayed unequivocally your commitment to this hospital time and time again. It was an easy decision. But I want you to know something." Dr. Rivas paused and leaned forward.

"I found a very interesting pattern--no, it's more like a peculiar pattern--in your background," he said before pausing, his lips clamped tightly with determination.

"Dr. Rivas, unless there is something in my background that calls into question my character or performance as a surgeon…"

"You don't have to talk about it, but I want you to know I have only one concern in appointing you to this position, and your new position won't do you any justice until you address one important factor."

"Whatever you may have discovered, I assure you it will not interfere with my performance."

"It already has. And it began long before you walked into the corridors of this hospital as an intern."

Dr. Rivas removed a piece of paper from his coat pocket and unfolded it. The handwriting was his, and Annah was relieved that whatever he'd found, he'd discovered the information on his own.

"You graduated valedictorian from high school at the age of fifteen, right?"

"Yes," Annah stated.

"That's quite unusual, don't you think?"

"It's not that uncommon. I was a high achiever as a child, and the competition to get into an Ivy League university for undergrad and a prestigious medical school was tough."

"This is true, but at fifteen years old, you also scored perfectly on your SATs."

"Again, I was a high achiever."

"Fine, but I find it hard to believe that you achieved a perfect SAT score from a high school rated as one of the nation's lowest in academic standards."

Annah could feel the moisture building on her palms, and her eyes avoided contact with his.

"As an undergrad at Yale, you took twenty-one units per semester, doubled your classes in the summer, and in two years graduated not just summa cum laude, but in every class you scored a perfect 100 percent. When you were accepted into Harvard Medical School, you managed to carry a full load, and you graduated number one in your class while working full time to put yourself through school. Your internship, residency, and fellowship here at New York University Hospital are superb. Now you are receiving an honor most doctors don't get until they are well into their forties. I have only one question," he said, leaning back in his chair. "Why are you hiding?"

Dr. Rivas knew Annah had already formulated an answer to his inquiry. He quickly put up his hand to stop her before she could speak. "This is a question for you to answer not for me, but for yourself."

Annah removed her hands from the medical records, where her sweating palms had left a visible imprint.

"I am honored that you have selected this hospital as your career choice," Dr. Rivas continued. "You are more than just a good doctor; you are a brilliant doctor. I have seen you work eighteen-hour shifts and go home and return in six hours and work through another twelve, and I know it's not out of your love for this place."

Dr. Rivas stood looking down at Annah, who stared at Christina's medical records. "The answer you are looking for is not within the four walls of this hospital. My advice, don't try to force your new position into being the answer."

Annah stood, extending her hand to Dr. Rivas, hoping to end his inquisition. "Thank you again for this opportunity to lead a fine team. And with all due respect, sir, I think I should leave now to begin my patient rounds."

"Well, with there being nothing else to say, congratulations, Dr. Kentwell," he said, resting his hand on her shoulder. "And Annah, I'm always here for you." His voice softened. "My office is being painted over the next two days, so have my assistant page me if you want to talk."

As Dr. Rivas left the boardroom, the one thing running through Annah's mind was not the promotion. Dr. Rivas had exposed what she tried desperately to keep secret her entire life. She was not just smart and a high achiever; she was a prodigy who had escaped life in a small farming town in Nebraska. Now her secret was in the hands of Dr. Rivas.

Leaving the boardroom, the hallways of the hospital appeared to her much narrower than normal. Coworkers smiled cordially at Annah in passing, or gave her a polite nod, but they never engaged her in conversation outside of her patient care or other hospital matters. They knew she was different, and Annah intentionally remained aloof. Never letting anyone get close enough to ask about her personal life became her branding. Her "secret" kept her from interacting with those around her. Practicing medicine fed her what she craved, and the thought of being without it made her feel anemic.

After graduating from medical school Annah had her sights set on a single goal, to practice medicine at New York University Hospital. The city's culture also appealed to her. The crowds and hectic pace enabled her to blend in and drown out the noise from her past that lurked in her subconscious. She wanted to forget Ashton, Nebraska altogether. Annah hoped and believed Dr. Rivas would keep her secret to himself. If there was one person she felt she could trust, it was him.

Before starting her patient rounds Annah passed through the cardiac intensive care ward and found herself in Christina's old room, staring at the empty hospital bed. *Death is so sweeping,* Annah thought. *So much is lost and nothing is gained.* Then the words of Christina's grandmother surfaced in the silence of the room. *"We will miss not knowing who Christina was to become."* The meaning carried by those words troubled Annah, and she could not understand why. But her logic always ruled her emotions, and dwelling any further on the statement by Christina's grandmother would be like poisoning herself. As she turned to leave, Annah could see Mr. Lee standing at the nurse's station and Irene pointing him in her direction.

"Mr. Lee? I would not expect you to be here," Annah said, leading him away from the room.

"Dr. Kentwell, I came here hoping to have a moment of your time."

"Yes, of course, Mr. Lee. How can I help you?"

"Our family will be leaving next week to fly Christina back to San Francisco for the funeral services. But before we leave the city, we're planning a small memorial on Thursday at our church. I wanted to personally invite you to come and celebrate Christina's life with us."

"Mr. Lee, thank you for the invitation, but I have two scheduled surgeries on Thursday and will be unable to attend. I offer you and your family my condolences."

"Very well then, again, thank you for everything." Mr. Lee turned to leave.

Annah knew she could not let him go without asking him one question.

"Mr. Lee?"

"Yes, Doctor Kentwell?"

"I need to ask you a personal question, if I may," Annah said, looking around to make sure no one would overhear the conversation.

"Yes, you may." Mr. Lee smiled, almost as if he anticipated her inquiry.

"Yesterday, when Dr. Rivas came to greet you and your family, you described me as someone who has carried a great wealth of knowledge since I was a child. What did you mean by that?"

Mr. Lee stepped closer to Annah, and this time she did not step back.

"I had a brother who was ten years older than I. When we were growing up as children in a small village in China, my brother excelled in areas well above his own age. For many days he would stay in his room and read books far beyond what most children his age could comprehend. We were very poor, and my parents did not understand how to raise a child who was so vastly different, and unfortunately, my brother could not handle the pressure of being unlike everyone else. At the age of sixteen he committed suicide. I was six years old when it happened. Our family was deeply saddened because he would be missed. But the main reason we were sorry was because he wanted to be the one to discover the cure for the rare cancer that would eventually take the life of our father. Had he lived, we believe he had the answer within him to find such a cure. You, Dr. Kentwell, have that same gift."

"What makes you say that?" asked Annah.

Mr. Lee looked past her into the empty ICU room. Tears began to well in his eyes.

"Because you grieve not for my daughter's life; you grieve because you need an answer to her death. And your mind will not rest until you find it."

He knows. Annah had only one recourse of action.

"I don't want to detain you, Mr. Lee," she said, cutting short their interaction. "But I have one other request before you leave. I ask that you keep our conversation today strictly confidential."

"Yes, of course. Have a good day, Dr. Kentwell," he said as he bowed and walked away.

Annah regretted asking Mr. Lee about what he said. It only intensified her desire to keep her life private. She appreciated the sentiment behind his statement, although personally she didn't support his belief in predestination and attempted to dismiss it. Or so she thought. Throughout the rest of that day she replayed the conversation with Mr. Lee over and over again, and for the first time she found herself distracted from focusing on the medical needs of her patients.

Later that afternoon when Annah ran into Dr. Sawyer, it finally dawned on her she had been promoted to chief cardiac surgeon. Dr. Sawyer walked toward Annah with the stride of a man much younger than his 69 years. It seemed odd he was retiring. He looked well preserved for his age, with the exception of the out-of-place gray hair on his dark brown African-American skin. People were often astonished when they learned how old he was, and it was a longstanding tradition when new interns came onboard to make bets to see who could guess his age. Annah was grateful she was selected for this role, but things had changed since the last time she'd spoken with him, and the closer he came, the more uneasy she felt.

"Dr. Kentwell, congratulations," Dr. Sawyer said, extending his hand. Annah placed both her hands in her pocket.

"Thank you, Dr. Sawyer, I'm honored for this opportunity." Annah remained stoic, fumbling for an item to fidget with in her pocket to help get her through the awkward moment.

"Doctor, it is customary to shake a person's hand when it is offered, especially if you are going to assume their position," he said diplomatically.

"My apologies, Dr. Sawyer." Annah shook his hand loosely, slightly embarrassed because of her sweaty palm.

"Well, if you have about an hour to spare, I would like to meet with you to begin our transition. There are some important things that need to happen over the next couple of months, and I would like to brief you on them."

"I just finished seeing my last patient, so now is a good time."

"Good. Let's get started."

Annah kept a distance between the two of them, but matched his long stride, hoping her endless sentences would mask her discomfort she felt over her handshaking. The hour-long meeting with Dr. Sawyer turned into four. It was approaching eight hours since she had eaten, but she found herself feasting upon Dr. Sawyer's vast experience, and was hesitant to interrupt him. Dr. Sawyer had made it clear he didn't want to overload her, but Annah's insatiable appetite for knowledge only increased as he talked, and she soaked it all in as if her brain were a porous sponge.

"Dr. Kentwell, it's 10:15. Don't you have something better to do than taking up my retirement time talking about medicine?" he joked.

"You're right. It's getting late, and besides, I volunteered to meet with two new residents at 8:00 a.m. tomorrow. But I am free after that."

"Tomorrow is Saturday, and you should be spending your spare time somewhere other than this place."

"How about Monday morning at 7:00?" she said, ignoring his comment.

"Dr. Kentwell, you already have the position. We can meet at 11:00. Besides, I'm an old man now and I need my rest. And so should you."

"Very well, 11:00 it is."

Annah talked nonstop with Dr. Sawyer about Christina's surgery, unaware they had taken the elevator to the underground physicians parking lot. Dr. Sawyer stepped out, expecting Annah to follow, but she stood inside the elevator staring at the almost empty, half-lit parking garage.

"You seem lost. Your car shouldn't be too hard to find. There are only three left," Dr. Sawyer said, holding the elevator door open for Annah. "Are you all right?"

"I'm-I'm fine. I just remembered that I must have left my keys in my office."

"You must be exhausted. Your keys are in your hand."

"Oh, yes, of course." Their voices echoed off the unobstructed concrete surfaces, and Annah whipped around as if someone were behind her.

"You seem nervous. Are you sure everything is all right?"

"Yes, please continue with what you were saying."

"I'd be happy to attend your case presentation on Christina." As Dr. Sawyer continued Annah's head was flooded by the sounds of her own silent screams, her legs weakening with each step she took toward her car. Beads of sweat formed on her forehead and the small of her back, and the car keys felt like slippery ice in her sweating palms.

"Doctor? Doctor? Are you sure you're okay?" he said as they arrived at the driver's side of her car. "You don't look well, and you are sweating profusely."

"Actually, I am starting to feel a little warm. I just need to hurry home and get some rest."

"You should not be driving in your condition. You'd better give me your keys and let me call you a cab."

"Really, Dr. Sawyer…" Before Annah could place the keys in her purse, Dr. Sawyer took them from her hand.

"Your eyes are fixed. Maybe we should head back into the hospital and have your blood drawn and see what's going on with you."

"No, Dr. Sawyer, there is no need for your concern," Annah said sternly. "I'm fine. Actually I'd like to take just a few moments…here…alone."

"I don't feel comfortable leaving you here alone. I'd better wait with you."

"I appreciate your concern, Dr. Sawyer, but it is not necessary. My keys, please," Annah said, holding out her hand and taking in deep breaths to slow her racing heart.

"You're sure you're okay?" Dr. Sawyer said, placing the keys back in her hand.

"Yes, I'm fine," Annah insisted. "I'm looking forward to our next meeting, Dr. Sawyer. This evening was very insightful." Annah turned away from Dr. Sawyer and pressed the remote to unlock her car. "Goodnight, Dr. Sawyer," she said in a curt tone.

"Very well then. Goodnight, Dr. Kentwell."

Annah hesitantly eased herself into her car and closed the door, the sound resonating in her mind as if she were being locked inside her own private prison. Her hands clutched the steering wheel as agonizing sweat poured from her palms. She tried to avoid looking into the backseat when for a brief second her eyes caught sight of a small blue silk button. Her eyes wandered just long enough for her to see more buttons scattered across the passenger seat. Then, on the floor of the car she saw her black skirt, torn from hem to waist. She clenched her eyes tight, but her mind played out what her eyes refused to see. She grasped the side of her neck where she could almost feel his mouth pressing close to her ear, his heavy breathing and deep voice butchering her thoughts. His dark skin matched the deep mahogany leather seats of her car, and his stench of urine, liquor, and cigarettes permeated her senses. She placed her hand on her inner thigh and could still feel the raised bruises. Sweat from her forehead rolled down the center of her face into her mouth, the salty taste reminding her of the foul rag he used to muffle her screams.

It wasn't until her mind regurgitated his vulgar profanities that she broke free of the horrendous flashback. Bolting from her car, she ran back toward the elevator. She frantically pressed the button, and as soon as it opened, she plunged inside and vomited as she collapsed on the floor. Hyperventilating, she fought hard to catch her breath so she would not pass out in her own filth. Her erratic breathing slowed down as she sat up and leaned against the back wall of the elevator, turning her face away from the reflection in the bronze-plated doors.

She'd done all she could to put the incident behind her. It had been two months, but her raw and exposed emotions made it feel like she had been raped all over again. She pushed the main lobby button, and by the time the elevator door opened, she had enough strength to stand and walk. Her ability to quickly regain her composure was an art she had mastered. Outside, the late-night breeze blew through her hair and began to dry the sweat from her face. She called the hospital and reported an incident in the elevator so it would be cleaned and aired before the next morning. It was almost 11:00 p.m., and now more than ever she anticipated the cab ride home to allow her time to think and process her next steps. Her experience in the medical field told her she needed to at least talk to someone about what had happened, but her stubbornness and pride superseded her logic. The flashbacks from the rape were becoming less frequent, and she believed her new promotion would occupy any idle time left in her schedule in which to ponder the event, the very thing Dr. Rivas warned against. She decided she would handle the rape just like she handled the other aspects of her life she despised: Leave it in the past long enough that it became irrelevant to the future.

She wondered how long before someone reported her abandoned new car to hospital security. Burning it was her first instinct, but an investigation from the insurance company would uncover the truth. She knew she would never drive it again, and Annah didn't care. As the cab crossed over the Manhattan Bridge, she threw the key to her car out the window, its trek to the bottom of the river yet another attempt to bury the memory of that gruesome event.

Annah unlocked the door of her condo and sighed heavily, relieved to be home. She undressed as she walked into the master bath adjacent to her bedroom, leaving a trail of clothing behind her, charging each article as if removing them would peel off the layers of shame and disgrace. She turned on the hot water in her spa tub and poured in her favorite bath oils of lavender and chamomile. The fragrant aroma filled the bathroom and became a healing balm, soothing her mind and emptying it of the events of the day. She was determined not to allow the flashback of the rape to deter her from the moment. She eased her body into the bathtub and took the soap-filled sponge in her hand and gently washed her back. Pausing, she pressed the palm of her left hand to her outer thigh and massaged the fading bruise. She only hoped that the memory would fade as swiftly. She was careful not to allow her eyes to see if any of the other bruises had disappeared. She believed sight unseen was the best course of action, for now.

As she relaxed her head against the back of the ceramic tub, her landline rang. She ignored it, until she recognized the voice of the person leaving a message on her answering machine. Before she could put on her bathrobe and get to the phone, she heard his last words, "She's gone." Annah stared at the phone before picking it up and pressing redial. She had purposely erased the number from her memory.

"Annah, is it you?" His voice was shaking.

"Yes, Edward." Annah could hear the shortness in his breath, as if he were fighting for his last words.

"She's gone, Annah. Your mother's gone, and I… we… need you to come home."

Annah's mouth would not form the words she felt in her heart. She wanted to say, "Thank you for letting me know," and then hang up. But she had no grudges against her father, Edward.

"When did it happen?" she asked reluctantly.

"About an hour ago. She went peacefully," Edward said, sniffling through his words.

"And Billy Joe, how is he?"

"Your brother's taking it pretty hard, but he's strong. We didn't want her to die alone, so for the past two days we've been taking turns sitting with her. I stayed and held her hand until she took her last breath. Annah…" Edward's voice grew weaker. "Your mother wanted you to know that…"

"Edward, don't do this," Annah said firmly. "She's dead now and there is nothing I can do."

"She loved you," Edward finished, his words conveyed intimately through the phone as if he were whispering a secret in her ear. Annah could feel his plea in the silence that followed. She was uncomfortable and knew he wanted a response, but she could only do what she had done for years, which was to remain emotionally dead. It was the defining quality of her relationship with her mother.

"I'll take a flight out tomorrow, and I'll call you when I land." Annah didn't wait for him to respond. She pushed the button on the phone to disconnect the call. The nausea rose again in the pit of her stomach, except this time it was different. Overwhelmed, she bolted toward the bathroom, reaching the toilet just in time. It seemed like minutes, but it was just seconds before the nausea returned, and she vomited the lining of her stomach. Feeling some relief, she laid her face on the cold tile of the ceramic floor, wishing she could as readily regurgitate the painful memories of her life in Ashton and her estranged relationship with her mother, Bethany. She sat up and opened the drain on the tub. Staring, she watched for several minutes as the water escaped without a trace. *"No one will ever know,"* she whispered as she massaged her abdomen.

She stumbled to her bed and lay across it in the still darkness. She covered her head with pillows as the mental remnants of the attack and her mother's death collided, fighting for equal attention. Reconciliation with her mother when she was alive was never an option. Annah believed that now that her mother was dead, Edward could finally put to rest his attempts to mediate their broken relationship. She took in deep breaths to settle the nausea. *"Two months,"* she said aloud. "It's not rocket science, just make a decision. You have your career to think about." The only reassurance Annah had was that her trip to Ashton would be two-fold. She would bury the feelings she had for her mother, and in making arrangements for an abortion she would bury the memory of the rape. Within minutes she was asleep.

Chapter Three

Ashton, Nebraska, was a small town of about 300 people, and as is the way in small towns, in which everyone knows everybody, secrets are exchanged like playing cards. Annah despised the town's insidious grapevine of gossip. As far as she was concerned, Ashton left much to be desired. No one was ever in a hurry, and for most of the day people spent hours at home making out whatever they could from the region's dwindling livelihood of agriculture. Other than the annual Polish Festival and acres of lush green fields, Ashton seemed oblivious to anyone and anything outside its borders.

Originally, her father inherited the 25-acre plot of farmland from his grandparents, but by the time Annah left for college, he closed the farm, and 22 of the 25 acres were sold to pay her mother's mounting medical bills. Annah was just three when her grandparents were moved into a nursing home to live out the rest of their days. The only story echoing from her past about her grandparents was that they died two months apart, such was their love for each other. Annah always felt it was just as well she couldn't remember anything else about her formative years with them. The less she recalled about her family, the more liberated she felt.

The two-hour drive from the airport gave Annah an opportunity to make follow-up calls to the hospital regarding her patient coverage. Dr. Rivas reassured her the hospital wasn't going anywhere and would be in the same place when she returned. He insisted that she take as long as she needed even though he knew nothing of her urgent need to leave.

Annah slowed the car as she came to the last stop signal before turning down the two-way, 50-mile-long road leading to the far countryside of Ashton to her parents' home. She accelerated through the intersection, and within minutes the scenery changed from city to country. When she was about halfway there Annah passed the combined middle and high school she'd attended. It was smaller than she remembered. The high school mascot of a farmer painted on the gymnasium wall was indicative of the type of people she grew up with. Graduating valedictorian from high school meant nothing to Annah. She didn't have any friends, and with no friends, she had no memories associated with the experience. Passing the landmarks of Ashton was like turning the page of a book she had been forced to read but never liked, hoping for a happily-ever-after to make up for the horrific storyline and its insignificant characters. Her homecoming only confirmed in her mind that she had made the right decision to distance herself.

The sun was sinking beneath the horizon by the time Annah reached the two-story ranch house she had grown up in. The towering maple tree that once shaded the front of the house had been cut down, leaving a large stump covered with an assortment of potted plants. The house had been painted brick red, a welcome change from the school-bus yellow Annah remembered, and flecks of white paint dotted the grass hugging the picket fence surrounding the remaining acreage. A slight breeze nudged the swing on the front porch, and the earthly fragrance of grass and wet dirt filled Annah's nostrils as she stepped out of the car.

"She's here!" her brother Billy Joe shouted, his boyish tone belying his nearly 35 years. "Savannah Grace Kentwell!" Without hesitating, Billy Joe rushed up and wrapped his hairy, burly arms around his sister and whisked her around in a circle as if she were a lost puppy who'd finally come home.

"Billy Joe! Put me down!" Annah asserted. "By the way, it's Annah, not Savannah."

"I don't care if you change your name to Yogi the Bear. You will always be my Savannah," he said, hugging even tighter before finally setting her down in front of the porch.

"You haven't changed one bit in all these years, sis, except that city food hasn't seemed to put any weight on your skinny bones."

The only picture her family had of her since she left home was her graduation photo from medical school, and she was now just five pounds heavier and her hair was shorter.

"A more appropriate word is willowy, Billy Joe," said Annah.

"Sure, and it's good to see you too, sis," he said sarcastically.

Annah turned to see Edward standing on the porch. The three steps he took towards her felt as if they covered miles. Her palms sweat as she extended her hand, hoping he would reciprocate. But instead she was met with Edward's embrace and his unshaven face pressing close to hers as he whispered faintly in her ear, "It's been too long."

Stepping back, Annah could see the tears nestled in the heavy wrinkles under his eyes. The straight, brownish-blond hair she remembered was now gray with traces of blond. His round face carried the marks of years spent in the sun, and his 6'2" portly stature bore the weight of the wife he lost.

"Let's go inside. I've made some sweet tea and bread." His voice stuttered.

"I'll get your bags out of the car, *Savannah*," Billy Joe said.

Inside, Annah was not at all surprised to find the décor and furnishings much as she'd remembered them. The country-style rustic furniture along with the bright calico colors of yellow, blue, white, and green swept throughout the living room, dining room, and kitchen. Each wall was overlaid, not with family portraits, but with tapestries made by her mother. Each one telling a story Annah had heard every day for the 15 years she lived in the house. The staircase leading to the bedrooms bore the same unfinished knotted pinewood railing. Time seemed to have come to a standstill in her parents' home since the day she left Ashton. Now that she'd returned, Annah wondered if the past would replay itself.

"It's been awhile since I've smelled fresh-baked bread," said Annah, walking into the kitchen.

"That's because you never venture outside the cell you call a hospital," Billy Joe teased, though Annah refused to engage him.

"Since your mother took ill four weeks ago I've been baking fresh bread every weekend. I guess I was just hoping one day she would come home," Edward said.

"She did, Dad, just a different home," Billy Joe said, patting Edward on the back.

Edward opened the oven door, and the smell intensified, permeating the room. He placed the hot bread on the table alongside a container of maple syrup and sweet tea. Annah studied him as he poured her tea.

"Edward, when is the funeral?" Annah asked.

"Well, I'm not sure. There are no other living relatives on your mother's side of the family. You remember my sister, your Aunt Faye? She and her husband are on their way now from Louisiana and should arrive Sunday afternoon. Your mother's condition prevented her from socializing much, and pretty soon the only other people who knew her were the caretakers in the nursing home."

Annah interjected, "So, likely we will have the wake or maybe even a small graveside service on Monday at 10:00, and I can book my flight out by Monday afternoon. And don't worry about the costs, Edward, I'll take care of everything."

"Savannah! It hasn't been twenty-four hours since our mother died, and you're already making plans to leave?"

"I have some important business I need to take care of, so I need to get back to New York as soon as possible."

"What's so important at the hospital that you can't stay a few days? Didn't you tell them what happened?" Billy Joe pushed.

Annah stared at the pitcher of sweet tea. "There's something in New York that requires my immediate, undivided attention."

"Isn't there some other doc who can cover for you?"

"Billy Joe, now don't harass her," Edward interrupted. "She's busy now that she's the new chief cardiac surgeon at the hospital, so just let it go."

Annah looked at Edward, surprised. "How did you know about that?"

"When the doctors said your mother was close to passing, I called the hospital looking for you. I spoke to a nurse by the name of Irene, and she told me all about it."

"No one told me you called."

"I didn't tell her who I was, and besides, I didn't want there to be a cloud on one of the most important days of your life."

"Chief cardiac surgeon? Wow, Savannah. That's impressive! I'm not surprised, though. You were always nerdy as a kid," Billy Joe said with a smirk.

"Annah, it would be good if you could spend some time with us. The circumstances are not what any of us would have chosen, but this is important. Besides, you have some relatives on my side of the family who have never seen you. And Billy Joe's kids would love to visit with their Aunt Savannah, especially after they've heard so much about you."

"Edward, I can't. I have to leave shortly after the services."

"Don't decide now. Give it some thought before you finalize your plans. Billy Joe, I'm sure your sister would like to rest after her long drive."

"I am a little tired," Annah said, yawning. "I think I'll lie down for a little while."

"Your old room is ready for you," said Edward.

"I need to get going," said Billy Joe. "Caroline is holding dinner for me, and I never miss a night tucking the kids in." Billy Joe leaned over the table and kissed Annah on her forehead. "It's good to see you, sis," he said, smiling. "Our kids will be thrilled to see that their Aunt Savannah really exists and she's not just a figment of our imagination."

"Annah, go on upstairs. I'll be up in a few minutes with your suitcase," said Edward.

One look at the staircase and Annah could feel the past drawing near, each step she took forcing it into the present. At the top of the stairs she froze and massaged her stomach hoping to eliminate the uneasiness. She walked past her parents' room and avoided looking inside. Billy Joe's old bedroom had been remodeled into a sewing room, and from the doorway Annah could see more of her mother's tapestries and needlepoint hanging on the bedroom wall. At the end of the long hall, her old bedroom was just as she left it. The dark brown door had faded, with traces of its former blue paint underneath. The college decals she had glued to the door panel had cracked with age. She placed her hand around the glass doorknob, her mind moving her backwards in time to the last argument she'd had with her mother.

"Savannah, what is this?" Bethany said, holding in her hand an envelope.

"It's my acceptance letter from Yale University," Savannah said as she continued stacking her books in the large oak closet of her bedroom.

"*So you've decided.*"

"*Yes, I have.*"

"*I guess it's settled, and there's no way your father and I can convince you to go to a local university here in Nebraska?*"

"*Mother, it's an old argument that I don't wish to re-visit. Yale is one of the top undergrad schools in the nation, and it's going to help me get into Harvard Medical School. Besides, I've already purchased my bus ticket. I'm leaving the day after graduation.*"

"*Then I suppose I should start planning your going away party.*"

"*That really isn't necessary, Mother.*"

"*Why? You are valedictorian, you are graduating two years ahead of your class, and you scored perfectly on your SAT exams—we've got quite a bit to celebrate.*"

"*It's you who wants to celebrate. I just want to leave this place, quietly, without having the whole town gawking at me for what anyone could have achieved.*"

"*Not just anyone, Savannah. You achieved it because you're a prodigy, and I think with a party we can celebrate your achievements and tell everyone what we've kept a secret in this family for too long.*"

"*I'm not a prodigy, I just studied harder than the other students.*"

"*Advanced Profusion Techniques on Bypass Surgery,*" Bethany said, handing Savannah the last book to put away. "*You are grossly disillusioned if you believe that's true. You are a prodigy, Savannah, and once you accept who you are, others will accept you.*"

"*Your speech is fifteen years too late. Besides, there is no one in Ashton like me, and frankly I'm tired of being alone.*"

"You are not alone. You have your family and friends here in Ashton."

"No, Mother! You still don't get it!" Savannah said as she slammed the closet doors shut. "I'm alone here! In this house, in this family! I'm not like you, Father, or Billy Joe! And to everyone else in this backwards town I'm just a freak of nature no one wants to be around! I'm tired of people laughing at me! And I'm tired of your attempt to change me into something that I'm not!"

"That's not true, Savannah. The only thing that I am guilty of is trying to get you to accept yourself and to love who you really are."

"No, you want me to change!"

"That is far from the truth."

"Really, Mother? Then why is it that almost every day when I come home from school you're sitting on the swing, waiting for me with that tattered old sewing basket to teach me a craft I have no interest in learning?"

"Because I wanted to give to you what my mother passed on to me."

"What? To learn how to sew and crochet!"

"It's more than that, Savannah. I'll show you."

"No thanks, Mother! My life is not going to be wasted like yours! I'm going away so I can become somebody and do something with my life, and that's certainly not going to happen here in this town of nobodies who spend their lives criticizing and judging others!"

"Savannah, calm down," Bethany said, taking her by the hand. "I'll make us some bread and sweet tea, and I'll get the sewing basket. Then we can sit on the swing, and I'll tell you everything you need to know."

"No, Mother! Let go of me!"

"Come now, Savannah," Bethany said, pulling Savannah by the hand.

"No! No! Why can't you just leave me alone, Bethany! Get out of my room and just leave me alone!"

"Bethany? Why did you call me Bethany?" she said quietly, letting go of Savannah. "I'm not Bethany, remember, I'm your mother."

"Just get out! I don't want any part of you or this place. When I leave, I am never, ever coming back!"

Bethany backed away, staring at the large tapestry over the bed. Savannah could see in her dazed eyes that she was slipping away. Her medication could only take the edge off her sudden mood swings, and after that, the only one who could manage her was Edward.

"You'll come back, Savannah. You'll come back. I'll go and sit on the swing with the basket and wait for you. You'll come back," Bethany said, smiling as she closed the door.

It was the last time Annah and her mother spoke, and she had no regrets. She turned the knob and opened the door to her bedroom. Her eyes were met with a blue-tinted scene as the full moon filtered its light through the sheer blue curtains of her favorite place, the bay window. She turned on the lamp on the nightstand next to the bed, her mind taking a mental picture of the room, comparing it to how it was the day she went away to college. It was just as she'd left it. The walls hung with pictures, banners, and posters of the six schools she was accepted to. The tapestry her mother made hung above the headboard. The bed linen, accessories, and décor of white, blue, and brown were the exact replica of a picture she saw in a magazine of a dorm on the campus of Yale University. She was eleven years old when she was able to finally convince her mother to redecorate her room from the unbefitting pink and white floral décor to the look of a campus dorm. The room smelled of freshly washed linens, and Annah suspected it was done in anticipation of her arrival. In the opposite corner of the room was a ceiling-to-floor closet. She opened the large oak doors and found that it, too, was just as she left it. There were advanced books on chemistry, math, physics, science, and biology. She could hear the echo of Dr. Rivas's voice. "*Why are you hiding?*"

"You remember them all, don't you?" Edward said, standing in the doorway holding her suitcase.

"Yes, I do," Annah responded softly.

"Ever since you were a toddler you had a thirst for knowledge."

"It hasn't changed," Annah said, thumbing through one of her old chemistry books.

"No doubt it hasn't. I recall once when you were two and I had come upstairs to tuck you in bed. You were sitting by the window, snuggled up in pillows, looking at this book about a rabbit. As I recall, his name was Peter."

"Mmm, I remember Peter Rabbit very well."

"I picked you up and you looked up at me with those big brown eyes and said, 'Father, why did Peter Rabbit eat the radishes and carrots in Mr. McGregor's garden when they didn't belong to him?' I had never read the book and thought you were making it all up until you turned to the exact page and pointed to the illustration and read the words to me. From that time forward we bought you as many books as we could afford. And when we couldn't buy books, we took you to the library, where you would spend hours reading. I think by the time you were twelve you must have read every book in the entire county."

"What was your impression when you and Bethany realized I was different from the other children?" Annah said.

"We did what most parents do when they find their child has a gift. We fed your passion."

"I wouldn't exactly say being a child prodigy is by any means a passion."

"Annah, you have been given an extraordinary gift. A gift many people would die to have."

"Well, it's not a gift, it's a burden. But I have come to terms with who I am."

"If you did, then more people would know than just your brother and me."

"My life is private and I like to keep it that way," she said, shoving the chemistry book back into the stack.

"It's not private. You've kept your life a secret, and I have respected the fact that you don't want the people you work with to know about Ashton. But there may come a time when you are going to need someone. Whether you accept us or not, in the end, your family will be the only ones there for you--and we won't judge you."

"I hate to disappoint you, but you are wrong. I don't need anyone. I got through childhood without Bethany's help, I graduated from college and put myself through medical school without anyone, and I don't need anyone, especially now, in my life." Annah stood back from the closet and leaned on her bedpost. She could feel the nausea rising with her emotions.

"Are you okay?"

"I'm fine."

Edward reached over and took Annah by the hand and felt her sweating palm. "It seems that your hand begs to differ."

"I don't want to be questioned about my life," Annah said, drawing her hand back.

"All right, no questions. Just talk to me."

"Edward," she sighed, "it's too complicated."

"If your mother was here she would tell you that..."

"Please, spare me the Bethany stories!"

"I just want to understand."

"That's just it. No one understands. I spent my entire childhood trying to be normal so I could fit in, and I ended up being miserable. And reading wasn't just something I loved. It was an escape to a place where the world made sense to me."

"Your mother and I both knew you were very special, and that one day you would find out what you are supposed to do with this gift you have been given," Edward said.

"Stop calling it a gift! If I had my choice, I would have wished this upon someone else just to have a normal childhood and life! I don't fit in and I don't belong here!"

"You don't have to fit in--you belong because we love you."

"If all I needed was for someone to say, I love you, I would not have put so much distance between me and everyone else for all of these years."

"Then why did you stay away for twenty-five years?"

"Because... because I have no connections here," Annah said, wrapping her arms around herself.

"We're your family. We're your connection," Edward said, stepping toward Annah, who turned away. "I wish I could change what happened between you and your mother, made your life here in Ashton better, but I can't and you can't either. Now that she's gone, are you going to continue to punish us? We were not the perfect parents, and maybe Ashton is not the ideal place to grow up, but we did the best we could with what we knew to raise you properly."

"I don't want to talk about this anymore," Annah said, massaging her stomach. "I'm tired and I need to get some rest."

"All right. The last thing I want is for us to argue. But before you retire for the night, there is something I have for you. I was going to wait until after the funeral, but I think you should have it now." Edward left the room and soon returned.

"Bethany wanted you to have this," Edward said, handing an old sewing basket to Annah.

"Why?"

"She wanted to give you the only part of herself she felt you would understand."

"Well, she was wrong. This is the last thing I want. I'm sure Billy Joe's wife Caroline can make better use of it than me. Just give it to her."

"Savannah, before your mother died…"

"Edward! Her efforts to reach me from the grave are not going to work. I just want to rest now."

"Okay, then I guess I'll just say goodnight. We'll talk tomorrow. Sleep well."

Edward set the sewing basket on the bay window. "Annah, I'm glad you are here. If you need anything, let me know," he said as he closed the door.

Annah walked over to the bay window and looked down. She could see the front porch swing slightly swaying in the warm night breeze. The squeaking sound of metal rubbing against metal brought back memories she thought were long buried. She envisioned Bethany sitting on the front porch swing. On her face, anticipation, on her lap, the sewing basket. She picked up the sewing basket and ran her fingertips over the worn and faded fabric covering the handles. The wicker basket was her mother's obsession. As her illness progressed, her crafts became her therapy. Every bed in their home had a homemade quilt. Every room had a needlepoint or a tapestry on the wall. And the kitchen was a marketplace of crocheted potholders and placemats.

Annah reluctantly unlatched the clasp on the basket and opened it. Everything she remembered was there: the crochet and knitting needles, yarn, and swatches of fabric. There were several new pieces of fabric cut in perfect squares carefully stacked by color, ready to be crafted into a quilt.

"Again, nothing has changed," she said aloud. Annah set the empty basket on the floor, noticing it was still weighty. She picked up the basket and pressed her hand along the bottom and could feel something bulky and square. She took one of the knitting needles and poked a hole through the lining and ripped the dry rot fabric apart. Underneath old swatches of fabric she discovered three leather-bound journals. She carefully removed them from the basket and noticed that each journal was discolored and warped. Water stains and scratches covered them, and an odd fragrance unlike leather emanated from the pages. The smell reminded her of the mornings she woke to the aroma of pumpkin pies and cornbread dressing baking on Thanksgiving Day.

"Well, it would be just like Bethany to pass on family recipes when she knows I don't cook," Annah said aloud. She opened the first journal and could not read past the first line. She read it over and over until finally coming to grips with what she held in her hand. She ran her fingers slowly over the words as if they were embossed on the pages, finally reading them aloud to hear what her mind strained to believe.

"This journal belongs to Kathleen Clarice O'Brien and is dedicated to Savannah. In the year of our Lord, 1798."

Outside the bay window the wind blew harder, moving the front porch swing even faster. It drew Annah's attention. The room was quiet and still. She turned off the lamp, and the moon's light settled serenely on the pages of the journal. She nestled her body comfortably in the pillows of the bay window and carefully turned the page.

Chapter Four

July 9, 1798

Charles and I are expecting any day the arrival of our first child. It has been a long-awaited journey for me. And just shy of a miracle from heaven that a middle-aged woman such as I would be married and conceive a child all within a year. My heart indeed is overwhelmed with joy as I anticipate the arrival of our baby and elated with the thought that Charles and I will finally become parents. Each day is welcomed as I have watched in nine months my body change and my appetite for food consumption double, and curiously, within the past week my energy has increased enormously. I am so grateful and pray that God will bless us with many more children before Charles and I retire to sitting in the rocker to live out our old age. Time has flown so quickly, for it seems like it was just yesterday we stepped onto the ship on a warm summer day to travel to this new land called America. Many on the boat complained about the long-anticipated journey; however, I relished every moment of the rocky seas and seemingly days upon end of landless sunsets. Even on the foggy cold day the ship docked, I carried the same unbridled spirit of anticipation as the day we left England, and I was determined to immediately regain a sturdy gait after our two-month voyage. Charles and I had very little to our name when we left England, just a few articles of clothing, and my mother's basket I carried filled with roots and spices that grew wild on our farmland back in Hillsboro, Scotland. The basket filled me with the sweet comfort of my mother's presence on the journey even though it has been years since she died. Yet I will never forget the days she spent intricately weaving and contouring the basket's shape. It was special to her as it is for me. I learned from my mother everything about how to grow and cultivate roots and spices for medicine. I have even created a number of remedies for coughs in ailing children. After our child is born I will be able to document this information. I thank my God and my mother for passing down this tradition and knowledge to me. I only wish that she were alive to witness the birth of her first grandchild. I will cherish all that she has taught me and follow in her footsteps, and I pray to God our children will do the same.

Life in the new land has indeed been far more than I could have ever imagined. Charles and I are now settled into a beautiful cottage in South Carolina. Although our abode is small, I will fill it with love and as many children as I am able to bear. South Carolina is home now, and I shall not look to the past—my life can only get better.

"Kathleen? Kathleen? Where in heaven's name are you?"

"I'm here, Sarah, upstairs, writing in my journal."

I could hear Sarah's heavy footsteps approaching the ladder that led up to the open floor of our small cottage. She placed one hand on her hip and grasped the ladder with the other while letting out a deep sigh, for she detested the climb.

"Heavens, Kathleen, you are due to have your son any day now, and it is beyond me why you insist on climbing up here just to sit and look out the window when you have perfectly good windows downstairs."

"I agree, my dear friend, but you cannot see what I see from up here."

Sarah was in her usual fussing mood. She and I had become quite the friends since we settled here shortly after we arrived nearly a year ago. Although she was a little more than half of my age, since I'd been with child, Sarah had been treating me like a sister, and I had grown rather fond of it given I had no siblings.

I watched Sarah's short, stocky frame struggle to climb the ladder, her pursed lips and raised eyebrows already poised to give me a stern talking to about how I should be in bed preserving my energy and what I should expect in giving birth. I couldn't decide what I found more amusing, watching Sarah struggle to climb the ladder or dramatizations of her exaggerated midwife experiences. Even though she had no knowledge that I had participated in delivering over 20 children, I felt as her friend it was more important that I entertain her concern for my well-being.

"If you give birth to your son in this loft, far be it from me to visit you, Kathleen Clarice O'Brien Hampton," said Sarah, out of breath as she reached the top of the ladder.

"Sarah, you must stop saying that I am having a male child. I could very well give birth to a girl, and it only lends credence to Charles's inexplicit proof that he can determine the gender of our child."

The Legacy

"But your husband did say that the firstborn in his family is always a boy, so it would be natural for him to conclude that his first child would be the same."

"It doesn't matter to me whether it is a boy or a girl. I just want to relish the fact that I am finally going to have a child."

"Your age has no significance in giving birth. It's about having the stamina to withstand the excruciating pain and long hours of labor. Besides, you are just forty-two years old, and I have delivered babies from women close to fifty years old."

"Your words comfort me," I said sarcastically.

"But it is true. Besides, the way you climb this ladder day in and day out, you have the energy to give birth to five children. So how many more sons shall you bear your husband?"

I knew where Sarah was going with her question, for she already had five children, and two were boys. I felt that underneath she wanted to see if I would be able to match her ability to be with child again within just a few months of weaning.

"Let us set aside this conversation, Sarah. Come and sit with me. I want to show you something."

"What is it? Have you uncovered another elixir?"

"No, but something just as good."

Outside the window of our cottage and beyond an oak meadow grew a cluster of small trees with purple blossoms. A few yards beyond the trees was a large clearing.

"Look, just beyond the purple blossoms. Do you see it?"

"See what, Kathleen? I see only a large barren landscape."

45

"Yes, that is it. Except it is not barren. I see a home, with many rooms to be filled with the laughter of our children. And beyond the house, land where I can plant and fill it with every type of root, vegetable, and herb to harvest. It is the place where I want Charles to build our new home. Just west of the oak tree, I dare say a half-mile's distance, there is a small creek where I can redirect its course so that our harvest will have an ample supply of water."

"How do you know this?" asked Sarah, offering a disapproving look.

"Yesterday, I walked the path for an hour to trace its source before turning back home."

"Kathleen! My God! What if you had stumbled, or even transitioned into birth, and with no one there... I dare not imagine what might have happened!"

"Sarah, Sarah, calm yourself. Women have been giving birth long before midwives were there to assist. I would have done what was natural. So there is no need for your alarm."

"Your tenacity amazes me at times. There are so many things you do that do not fall within the norm of a woman's role. Are all women like this where you are from? If so, I envy you that."

Sarah's envy was not just of my own life. She envied anyone who lived outside the four walls of her home. It was well known that Sarah took every opportunity to attend to everyone else's affairs while her servants took care of her five children and household matters. Sarah had a reputation as the town's noble social butterfly. No one seemed to mind that she was a busybody, as she was well liked by everyone. My aptitude for adventure and going outside the boundaries of perceived roles of a woman not only fueled her envy but exposed how unhappy she really was with her own life. Sarah was submissive and I was obstinate.

"I tell you what, Sarah. Why don't you join me the next time I venture out on a walk. That way, in case I do transition into childbirth, you will be there to assist me."

"Oh, I would be delighted!" Sarah said, throwing her arms around me as if I had granted her a wealth of money.

"It would be my pleasure. But for now it is time," I said.

"Goodness!" Sarah shrieked. "The child is coming!"

"No, Sarah. It is not *that* time," I said calmly. "It is time for me to go downstairs and prepare the elixir that I promised to Mrs. Tanner. Her eight-year-old daughter, who has been ailing for a number of weeks, is in need of a suitable cure. Mrs. Martin's daughter had a similar cough and my remedy worked perfectly."

"Word is indeed getting around about you, Kathleen. You should be very proud about the way you have made yourself a household name in our town."

"I do not seek nor am I pursuing a name. I am doing only what is natural."

"We'll, what you call natural to some is somewhat odd to others. In America, we are accustomed to the husbands creating the image for the family. You have surpassed that. Your name is spoken of around town as if you had no husband at all."

"Sarah, you should never lend your ears to idle gossip. It could do irrevocable harm."

"But it's not gossip, Kathleen. It is truth. Everyone has been taking about how you have a gift to heal ailing children."

"It's not a gift, Sarah. It's just some old family recipes passed down through the generations. We had very little when I was growing up in Scotland, and my mother used what we gathered from the earth to cure our ailments."

"Be that as it may, your name has succeeded your husband's, and I find it rather daring."

"I'm not trying to succeed Charles or anyone else for that matter! I only want to help those who are hurting. Besides, success should never be measured by a person's notoriety or wealth. It's character that is first and foremost. As for my husband, we both jointly share in this child as well as any success, be it his or mine."

I had never spoken sternly with Sarah before, and my reaction indicated she had struck an area of sensitivity. I knew very well the townspeople were talking. They were curious as to how a woman with no formal education knew how to treat and cure the sick. Before Charles and I arrived in South Carolina, the blacksmith served as doctor. But in truth he could no more cure an aliment than I could affix shoes on a horse. Once word was out that my elixir had cured one child of her cough, the townspeople, all except for Sarah, kept me at a distance. It seemed to be the story of my life--and of my mother's.

"Sarah, let's not..."

"I know, I know. Let's not consider this conversation any longer. It's your Scottish way of telling me not to pry any deeper into your personal life. Truly, Kathleen, you are an enigma, and above all a delightful friend. Come, I'll make us some tea and you can tell me more." Sarah smiled to soften the moment.

When Sarah and I reached the bottom of the ladder, we were startled by a myriad of screams coming from the front of the cottage.

"Who could that be?" I said to Sarah.

"It sounds like Victoria Livingston."

I hurried to the front door and opened it to find Victoria carrying four-year-old Elizabeth in her arms. Victoria's eyes reflected what any mother's heart would.

"Kathleen!" Victoria stammered. "Elizabeth's not breathing! She's not breathing! Why is she not breathing?"

I took Elizabeth from her mother and laid her on the floor. "What happened, Victoria? Hurry, tell me what happened!"

"I-I-I was in the kitchen and had just given Elizabeth some chicken pie, when she said…"

As Victoria struggled to finish her sentence I placed my ear to Elizabeth's chest. I could hear her heart beating. She was somehow getting some air. I opened her mouth and reached in and discovered a large object blocking her airway.

"There is no time to waste," I said. "Sarah, in my garden there is a plant with dark purple leaves. I need several of them, now! Victoria, I need a large bucket of water from the well. Quickly! Both of you, there is not much time!"

With Sarah and Victoria out of the room, I could focus on what I needed to do. I grabbed Elizabeth by the heels of her feet and turned her upside down. I struck her with two quick sharp blows to the upper back. A thin, flat piece of bone flew out of her mouth and onto the floor. Elizabeth let out a muffled cough. Seconds later, a cry that summoned Victoria and Sarah back into the house. Victoria grabbed Elizabeth from my arms, smothering her in kisses and hugs.

"She's going to be okay, Victoria," I said.

"But what happened? What did you do?"

"Yes, Kathleen, what *did* you do?" Sarah said, never taking her eyes off of me.

"You should take little Elizabeth home now, Victoria, and put her to bed quickly," I said, stroking Elizabeth's hair. "She needs to rest now. Sarah, why don't you accompany Victoria." Sarah didn't move, and I knew she wasn't going to leave until she had some answers.

"Victoria, I will accompany you shortly," Sarah said, leading her to the door. "I need to make sure that Kathleen is feeling settled after this experience."

"Kathleen, I cannot possibly thank you enough," said Victoria, holding on to Elizabeth as if her life depended on it. "If you had not been here… I just want you to know how grateful our town is to have you here. You are indeed an exceptional woman."

"You are welcome, Victoria. And you, little Miss Elizabeth, you must be careful from now on what you put in that tiny mouth of yours." Elizabeth smiled and I kissed her cheek. I closed the door, only to turn and face Sarah, who stood with her hands on her hips ready to commence an investigation.

"Kathleen, you sent us out of the room because you did something you did not want us to see. And don't say to me, 'Enough of this chatter.' I want to know exactly what you did, and I won't leave until you tell me."

"This event has tired me and I need to lie down and rest. I really can't explain to you what I did or how I knew what to do. What is more important is that a mother has her healthy little girl back. And standing here posturing to me will not change my mind, Sarah. All that matters is that she got Elizabeth to me in time."

"All right, I will not interrogate you." Sarah relaxed her stance and placed her hands in mine. "But you need to know something. The people in our town are going to hear about what you did today for Elizabeth, and once again you will be the talk of the town. Some people will marvel, but I know our townsmen very well. The majority of them will see it as peculiar. So, whatever the reason you and Charles came to South Carolina, I am glad you are here and I am glad to call you my friend. Get your rest, my dear. I will come after the dinner hour to see that all is well with you."

"You are indeed a true friend," I said, hugging Sarah. I watched from the window of our cottage until she disappeared down the narrow path leading to her home. "*Peculiar*," I said aloud. I had no choice in the matter of saving Elizabeth's life. I could not have allowed her to die to avoid being exposed. I remembered what my mother had to endure, and I was not ready to face the same reproach from people who would only judge me by their fears.

I placed my hand on my stomach. I could feel the baby turning, my womb contracting, and the unusual sensation of my body tightening and relaxing. For a brief moment the incident with Elizabeth was far away. I gazed at the ladder and decided to make one last climb, for I was sure the baby would come by the end of the week. Each step upward brought a sense of peace. I sat at the window and took in a deep breath, allowing my mind to run free without any restrictions or distractions. Caressing my stomach, I wondered if my own child would be peculiar just like me. Or if my child would live in seclusion, fearing someone would see his or her difference as evil or something divine. I'd kept this very secret from Charles for fear of the same. I often wondered how he would feel if he knew about my abilities. I had no idea if Charles would be threatened by my peculiarity or embrace it.

I opened the latch to the window and a breeze carried the herbal fragrance from my garden. It warmed the empty room. I closed my eyes, and visions of running through Scottish fields as a child enraptured me. I could hear my mother's voice, laughing as she ran to catch me, her curling red locks reflecting against the sun and golden wheat fields. When she caught me I would inhale the fragrance that lingered on her hands and in her hair from the spices she used in preserving our food for the upcoming winter months. I would never forget the aroma or my mother, Clarice O'Brien. We were each other's only best friend and confidante.

I sighed heavily at the thought of having to tell Charles. *As soon as the baby is born, I will tell him. He must know this about me. He must know the knowledge I have is to help others and not to harm them. I cannot hide anymore.*

Chapter Five

I could tell dawn was preparing to arrive from the smell of coals burning in the furnace of the town's blacksmith. From our bedroom window I saw a glimmer of candlelight coming from the kitchen of the Henderson's home. The scent of bacon and bread made its trek every morning to our cottage. I looked over at Charles sleeping, the smell arousing his slumber. He took in several deep breaths as if trying to consume the food through his nostrils. At the age of 52, Charles was still a very handsome man. His thinning salt-and-pepper hair did not compare to his full, broad shoulders. When he stood erect, he was almost a foot taller than most men, and he had a deep, velvet voice that commanded the attention of anyone within earshot. With one more deep breath, Charles exhaled and opened his eyes.

"Why are you out of bed?" he said in a muffled whisper. "Is the birth of my son upon you, my beloved?"

"No, my love, but the day will be soon."

"Then you should be resting."

"True, but I'm too excited. I have mixed emotions. I will miss carrying our child, but also I am ready to welcome it into this world."

"Then you should be sparing your energy, for once he arrives things will change."

"Charles?" I hesitated. "I've been thinking about something."

"What is it, Kathleen?" Charles said as he sat up in bed.

"Most women give birth to their first child at a young age. And I have witnessed many women my age who have lost their lives because their bodies were not strong enough to endure the pain and the difficulty of labor. If this should be the case for me and you are given a choice between saving our child's life and saving mine, I want you to put the life of our child first."

Charles arose and walked over to the window and stood behind me. He wrapped his large arms around my waist and his hands covered my belly as if he were charged to guard it. He whispered in my ear, "You need not ever be concerned. No harm will ever come to my son."

"You mean our child?"

He slowly turned my face toward his. His silence spoke more than a thousand words.

"Yes, our child," he said coldly, kissing my cheek.

"I should not have burdened you with such insignificant concern, my love," I said, turning away from him. "You should go back to bed and get your rest."

"It's nearly dawn. Perhaps I'll dress now and go down to the mill. It will give me an early start. And you?"

"I… I want to take a walk through my garden and gather some fresh herbs. When I am finished, I will prepare your morning meal."

The rising sun peered through the large trees that hovered over the cottage. I lingered for a moment and watched Charles gather his clothes to dress for the day. It was evident. He wanted a son. I wondered what kind of father he would be if our child was a girl. The fact he was so sure our child was a boy could not escape me. As soon as I dressed, I headed outside, anxious to step into the place of my own hallowed ground. With my bare feet planted inches beneath the dew-drenched soil, I felt an immediate connection. A mystery even I could not understand.

"The earth is the Lord's, and the fullness thereof" are the words my mother would say each time she went into the fields to plant for the harvest. I buried my feet deeper into the soil. It was easy for me to lose myself in this place. I closed my eyes and absorbed the rejuvenating morning rays, my mind going back to when I was a child. At three years old I learned how to pull roots from the ground at the right time. My mother would brew them in a large kettle in the fireplace as I sat on a stool next to the blaze and inhaled the heavenly scent. Nothing measured, nothing preset, instinct was her only guide. My mother had an inner knowing of what other spices and ingredients to mix. After hours of preparation, she would carefully pour the brew into several bottles and label them for what she knew would help certain ailments. Then she would wrap the containers in burlap and root leaves and bury them deep in the ground where no sunlight or water would degrade their contents. Softly I caressed my stomach. All this knowledge I have to pass to my child, be it male or female. I thought Charles worthy to be a father of our children. But now I couldn't help but wonder what would become of our child if I didn't bear the son he desired.

During our morning meal Charles remained silent and his eyes never left the plate of food in front of him. I had not known him long enough to gauge all of his expressions, but I knew that something weighed heavily on his mind, as the impending birth of our child weighed heavily on mine. At this moment I regretted not taking the time to get to know him better. After a one-week courtship Charles insisted that we get married right away; starting a family was to soon follow. I presumed that, given our age, it was the prudent thing to do, and I had no objections. During the courtship I told him about my life, my family, and why I was sent to England. In return, Charles excited me with his desire for building a home, raising a family, and being a good God-fearing provider. He told me very little about his past other than the fact that he lost both his first wife and his son when she was giving birth. I wanted to live in his home in England, but he convinced me the home, as well as England, carried too many painful memories and it would be better for us to begin our new life in America. Perhaps his preoccupation on having a son was because of the devastation he experienced with his first family. I only hoped this to be true.

"Charles?" I said, breaking our silence. "The baby will be here soon. I'd love to talk about the plans to build our new home."

Charles looked up at me with empty eyes. He took the napkin from his lap and slowly wiped his mouth.

"You said we would talk about this once we were settled here," I said, studying his distant expression.

"Yes, I remember."

"I took a walk through the wooded area across the way, and there is a creek with fresh water which flows for at least an hour's walk."

"You walked alone?"

"Why, yes." I continued. "I think it would be an excellent place to build our home, and with a little work we can divert the creek so we will have plenty of water for my garden."

"Kathleen, my child will need his mother to care for him and not waste her time on watering a garden, let alone wandering to places unbefitting for a woman."

"What did you say?"

"I said, our child will need..."

"Charles. You keep referring to our child as yours."

"Kathleen," he said, pushing his plate away. "Your place is here, tending to me, our home, and child."

"I will do that, but I also want to tend to my garden. You know how important this is to me."

"You can hire servants to care for and till the land. Your life will be filled with household matters and raising the child."

"Is this all I am to do, Charles?"

"This is all you will need."

"I need more."

"I should say that your being with child has caused you to become irrational and irreverent. These traits I presume will cease after the child is born. We will not speak of this matter anymore. I'll be home by supper. If the child comes, have Sarah's son Jacob find me near the mill."

My wide eyes burned as they filled with tears, but my stubbornness kept me from wading in self-pity or wasting tears on Charles. I stood at the front of the cottage and watched Charles disappear on his horse down the path toward the mill, along the way seemingly trampling underfoot all my plans, hopes, and dreams for the future. Something had changed in my husband. At first it was subtle, and when it surfaced I told myself that we just needed time to get adjusted to our new surrounds. But in reality, Charles's adamancy for a male child was there all along, each day of the pregnancy bringing me closer to the truth, and finally unveiling the mask he had been wearing since our first encounter. How could I have allowed myself to be deceived? I cradled my abdomen as if I were holding my child in my arms. *No time for tears.*

"You deserve more," I whispered. "And more you shall have."

The dust settled on the trail Charles took to the mill, and I could see Sarah waving as she hurried her steps toward the cottage. The closer she came the less able I was to hide the disdain I felt for Charles.

"What is it, Kathleen? Are you well?" Sarah pressed.

"Aye," I responded.

"I don't believe you. I saw Charles heading away from here, and he neither acknowledged nor greeted me as he passed. Is there something you want to tell me?"

"Sarah, there is nothing to discuss."

"Then tell me about the strange gentleman standing behind the oak tree. Is he the source of the trouble you do not wish to speak of?"

"I have no idea who he is."

"I'd better have Jacob fetch Charles from the mill so he can approach the gentleman."

"No, I'll handle this myself."

"Kathleen, you don't know what type of person he is."

"I don't care. And whoever he is, he shouldn't be trespassing on our property."

"Let us go inside and wait. Maybe he will just leave."

"No, Sarah. I want to know the nature of his business."

"But it is not appropriate for a woman to undertake matters with a stranger. Leave it to your husband or I can have the blacksmith approach him."

"I don't need a blacksmith," I said firmly.

"You should not do this alone in your condition, Kathleen, I implore you. Let us go inside."

"Sarah, I have a chill. Please go inside and retrieve my shawl for me."

"I know your tactics," she said with a sneer. "You are indeed one remarkable but stubborn woman, Kathleen Clarice O'Brien Hampton. I have only one request."

"What bargain do you put before me now?"

"Just make sure you tell me every detail of your encounter with him."

I waited until Sarah went into the cottage before I headed through my garden toward the stranger. From a distance he looked to be in his mid-forties, and judging by his clothing he was poor. As I approached him he reached into the ground and pulled up a root. He wiped it on his dusty black coat and ate it as if it were a delicacy to his impoverished appetite.

"I've seen you before, haven't I?" I said.

"Your memory is accurate, madam," he said, his accent bespeaking one raised on rural King's English. Without even looking in my direction he pulled up another root, this time shoving it into his pocket.

"Apparently you have no fear of being punished for stealing or else you would cease taking what is not yours."

"One cannot be charged as a thief if he steals from himself," he said, walking toward me as he pulled up another root and placed it in his pocket.

"You're not afraid of me, are you?" he said, wiping the residue of dirt from his lips.

"Should I be?"

"Perhaps if you knew who I was you would think different."

"I don't know you, but I have seen you before."

"And I you."

"Now I remember. You were in England. The day Charles and I married, at the home of my aunt, you stood outside watching from across the way. And again when Charles and I boarded the ship to America, you were there on the docks, watching us depart."

"I see Charles has married a woman who is very observant."

"How do you know Charles and why are you here?"

"On the contrary, madam. The question you should be asking yourself is do *you* know Charles and why are *you* here?"

"You can cease your riddles and answer me immediately."

"Ah, I see my brother has yet to tame your tongue, my dear *sister-in-law*."

"Sister-in-law? Charles has no brother! He is an only child."

"I'm not surprised he hasn't told you about me. But you are not alone. He didn't tell his other wives about me either."

"Wives? That's preposterous. There was only one wife before me and she died giving birth."

"I see my brother has succeeded in concealing the real truth about himself."

"Sir, you share no truths! Only lies in an attempt to gain something monetary for your poverty."

The gentleman approached to within an arm's length. Up close I could see he and Charles shared the same physical features. He was shorter than Charles, and through his unkempt facial appearance I noticed Charles's deep blue eyes.

"You and I both have something to gain from my presence here."

"Sir, I have nothing to gain, and neither am I in the least provoked by your presence. You may leave at once," I said, turning away from him.

"Am I to understand then, madam, that you do not wish an answer to my riddles? And that will you walk away pretending this incident never occurred?"

"How do I know you are telling the truth?" I said, turning back toward him and planting my feet firmly in the soil.

"Then answer me this. When you found out that you were with child and told my beloved brother, was not his response that his child will be a male?"

"It is not unusual for a man to want a male child first."

He stooped down and filled his hand with the damp soil and inhaled its fragrance.

"This garden, it is your doing, correct?"

"Yes. It is."

"Then my brother's tactics for pursuing females who come from a lowly farm background remain firm. For your first encounter with Charles did he not say, 'I believe that your roots should be planted in our garden?'"

I could feel my heart pounding inside of my chest, for those were the very words Charles had used. I covered my mouth to disguise my astonishment.

The man stood. "Do not be alarmed, my dear sister-in-law," he said sarcastically. "For I am here to warn you, not to harm you. Charles is not the man you think he is. He wants a male child for one reason and one reason alone."

"Why? What has he done?"

"It is not what he has done, but more so why he did it. You see, my beloved relative, Charles and I are the only remaining heirs to our uncle's fortune, and it is stipulated in our uncle's will that 25 percent of the estate will be divided amongst Charles and myself, but the other 75 percent of the estate is granted to either one of us whose wife bears a legitimate firstborn son."

"Why would your uncle sanction such a despicable decree?"

"He wants to ensure that our family's legacy remains for generations to come."

"Then it is pretentious for your uncle to believe he can pass down a legacy to a person without character."

"It is forthright that my family's reputation will long precede its deranged character, but a very rich and deranged individual one of us shall be."

"I don't care about your family's name or its wealth. I am concerned about the life of my child."

"Then let the truth speak for itself. If you bear Charles a daughter, both you and your daughter will not survive."

"Charles would not harm me... He loves me."

"Madam, no need to try and convince me of his love for you. Charles has lived many lives you know nothing about. That should witness his lack of love for you. He has told you the story about losing his wife and son during childbirth?"

"Yes, he told me the accounts of his loss."

"And he told you he wanted to come and start a new life here because of the pain and grief he associated with living in England?"

"Yes, that is also true."

"What he told you is a pale version of the truth. The whole truth is his wife gave birth to a girl, and three days after the child was born, his wife and the child mysteriously died. Adeline, the wife he told you about, was his third wife. Did he forget to tell you about his second wife, Meredith, who suffered an accidental death after giving birth to twin girls, and how the twins managed to contract a fatal disease and died weeks later? And surely Charles has told you about his first wife, Emma, and her encounter with death? How much more truth would you like to hear! Do you not see the pattern!"

"Stop it! Stop it! I don't want to hear any more! You are to leave this place immediately and never return!"

"Be that as it may. Now that you know the truth, you have only one option." He stood back and tipped the dust-covered hat he wore, turned, and walked down the path that led away from the mill.

Sarah came from the house, out of breath from searching for my shawl, which I knew to be obscurely hidden.

"I found your shawl hidden underneath your comforter, but you probably knew it was there all along."

"I'm sorry, Sarah. I must have left it there last night."

"Now tell all. What did the stranger want?"

"He... he was looking for the person that once lived in the cottage, years ago."

"It must have been a long time ago. The cottage was empty for almost three years prior to you and Charles taking possession."

Sarah and I stood and watched until he disappeared out of sight. My heart weakened. The irony was all too similar--Charles had secrets from his past he wanted to keep from me, and I had a secret from my past I wanted to share. The reality of my circumstances overwhelmed me. My thoughts became erratic. I felt an unusual weakness in my body as if the blood were being drained from the very life of me. A sharp pain pierced my back and reached around into my lower extremities, where an intense pain flowed throughout my entire body. Fluid spilled from me and soiled the ground. It was time.

Chapter Six

"Kathleen, come, we need to get you to bed immediately."
Sarah's calming voice instantly gave me an assurance that
I could follow her directions. As I entered the cottage, the
pain became intense and it was even more difficult to walk.

"Oh God!" I yelled.

"Here, put your arm around my neck," Sarah insisted.
She was shorter than I, but as I leaned upon her Sarah easily
carried my weight.

"Sarah, I hate to admit it, but this is not what I had
expected it would be like, and I am a bit apprehensive."

"Kathleen, it's fine to be afraid." She smiled. "You will
always have my utmost respect. And I promise you that I
won't tell a soul. I never tell the secrets of those I hold in
high regard."

"Then it truly speaks volumes about our friendship. I'm
glad you are here."

"Rest assured, I'm not going to leave your side. As soon
as you are settled I will have Jacob find Charles and tell
him to come home immediately. He will not want to miss
hearing the first cry of his child," Sarah said with excitement.

"No! Charles must not be here."

Sarah hesitated as she helped me into bed. "Kathleen, you are just nervous. It is to be expected. But everything will be fine."

"You don't understand. Charles cannot be present at the birth of my child."

Sarah stopped as she helped me remove my outer garments. "This is the first I have heard you specifically refer to the baby as your child. Something has changed?"

"I can't tell you any more, but you must believe me. Charles must not be here. It is crucial that he not know when the child is born." My words were short and sharp in between my heavy breathing. Sarah could see the plea in my eyes as she held my hand. I squeezed her hand tightly and released it as several deep groans of pain escaped me.

"Why is this so crucial? Why don't you want him here?"

"My-my life is in danger."

"Danger? What harm would come that Charles cannot protect you from?"

"Sarah…" I paused as the pain began to subside. "What I'm going to share you must swear to me never to tell a soul. No matter what anyone says, you must promise me you will tell no one what takes place here in this room."

"I swear to you, Kathleen, I will not tell a soul. You can trust me."

"The man I spoke to in the garden… he is Charles's brother, and he brought me news. Charles had three other wives prior to me, and each of them had children. All of them daughters. The children as well as the wives mysteriously died days after giving birth."

"Oh my goodness, then it is true!"

"You know of this matter?" I panted.

"It is a rumor we have heard for many months, but the nature of it did not lend itself to be truthful that a man would do such harm. But I see it is no hearsay."

"Tell me what you know."

"It was six months prior to you and Charles's arrival. It was said there was an elderly gentleman who was an heir to a great fortune, but the only way he would receive his inheritance was to produce a male child."

"Where did this man reside?"

"In England. Kathleen, this rumor must be of your husband Charles!"

"Sarah, I beg of you, help me! Please! I don't care if I die. I will do anything to save my child's life! I can't allow Charles to have my child! I cannot allow this treachery to continue!"

Sarah cupped my face in her hands. "He will not have you, nor will he have your child, I swear my life on it."

I smiled. The pain intensified.

* * *

The voices in the room were faint at first and I could not make out the words, but the sound was familiar. I slowly opened my eyes to see Sarah standing over me. To my relief she placed a cold towel on my forehead, and with another towel she wiped my face and neck.

"Kathleen, how are you feeling?"

"I'm tired and thirsty," I whispered through my parched throat.

"You have rested well."

"Sarah?"

"Shhh, there is no need for you to speak," she replied, placing her fingers on my lips. I felt the coldness of a familiar hand holding mine. I turned my head and looked into the eyes of a man I wished I had never known. Charles lifted my hand to his lips and kissed it gently.

"Where is my child?" I said, withdrawing my hand from Charles.

"No questions, you must continue to rest," Sarah said.

"Where is my child?" I pleaded. Sarah lowered her head to avoid making contact with my eyes.

"I'm sorry, Kathleen."

"Sorry? Sorry for what?"

"Kathleen, I don't know how to tell you, but she did not survive."

"She? But my child did survive. I distinctly heard a baby crying. Where is she?"

"You have had a fever for several hours now. You only hallucinated you heard the cry of a child."

"It is true." Charles nodded.

"Sarah? Please tell me it is not so!"

"I'm sorry, Kathleen."

"What happened?"

"She didn't have a chance," Sarah said. "She was born with the cord wrapped around her neck. There was no life in her by the time she came from your womb."

"All lies! I want to see her now! Bring my child to me this instant!"

"Kathleen, calm down. What Sarah said is the truth. Don't you remember?" said Charles.

"I think the fever has impaired your memory. You just need to rest a while longer," said Sarah.

"Sarah, you are my friend. Please, please tell me…"

"Well, your time was very difficult and you were in a lot of pain. But there was nothing I could do. I told you she was stillborn. You were angry and enraged. I tried to comfort you, but you said that no one, not even Charles, would lay eyes upon her."

"Where is she?"

"You said that you did not want the image of her death to remain with you the rest of your days. Then you demanded that she be cremated along with all that came from you, including the soiled bed linen."

"Lies! All lies! How could you, Sarah? I trusted you!"

"I did only as you requested."

"I would have never made such a request!"

"Kathleen, Sarah acted in your best interest. By the time I arrived from the mill, it was all done. Only her ashes are left," said Charles.

"What preposterous lies you two have crafted!"

"I didn't want to do it. I suggested that you wait and give Charles an opportunity to see his daughter."

"Show me her ashes, now!" I said angrily.

"Kathleen, you are weak and you should rest," Sarah said, forcing me back onto the pillows.

"I shall not rest until I see my child's ashes! Show them to me, immediately!"

"Kathleen… she is gone," said Charles.

"And you, Charles. You do not mourn the death of our daughter?"

"The death of our child will always be revered, but I cannot mourn that which I have never seen or known."

"I am so sorry for your loss, Kathleen," Sarah said.

"Sarah, you have served Kathleen well today. You have only done what she wished, and you will not be held responsible for any of your actions. Now, I'm sure that you need to see that your own household is cared for. You may leave," Charles said.

"But who will care for Kathleen? She has suffered a tremendous loss and she still bleeds."

"I will care for Kathleen myself."

Sarah could see the fear in my eyes, pleading for her to stay. I took her by the hand and squeezed it firmly.

"Before I leave, I'd like to make sure that she is healing well. She lost quite a bit of blood, and I want to see that her womb is closing properly."

"That won't be necessary. I am very capable of caring for my wife. Should she need you, I will be sure to find you."

"Kathleen, rest well," Sarah said, letting go of my hand and kissing my forehead.

Charles sat on the bed next to me. His gaze wandered, never looking me in the eye. "I'm glad she is gone. I have been waiting for you to awaken. Sarah made you some of your special healing tea. I'll heat it and bring it to you. She said it would promote a fast recovery."

"Charles, I'm not ready to drink anything, not yet. This news has left me melancholy. I'd like to be alone for a few hours."

"Of course, I understand. You have suffered a tremendous loss. I need to make one last trip to the mill before sundown. When I return, I will prepare you a meal and some tea." When he reached over to kiss me, I turned my head aside.

"I'll rest until you return."

I waited in silence to hear the hoofs of the horse carry Charles away from our cottage. My breathing could not keep up with the pace of my heart. I only hoped Sarah was waiting close by to return. It would be dark by the time Charles returned, and we needed every second of daylight.

Three hard knocks on the front door startled me. I sat up in bed and was able to rise to my feet. Even before I reached the bedroom door Sarah met me and enveloped me in her arms.

"I saw him leave. Are you well?"

"I will be able to rest when I know I am safely away from Charles. But we must move quickly. Charles will return soon from the mill. Did you prepare everything?"

"Yes, the horses are well fed, and the wagon is filled with supplies for a three-week journey."

"Where is the wagon?"

"It's just beyond the path where the creek begins to change course toward the south."

"What about my roots and spices?"

"You would be pleasantly surprised that I took the containers from your kitchen and replaced them with grass and wild flowers just in case Charles decided to look inside."

"You are an intelligent woman, Sarah," I said, smiling and hugging her. I opened the cedar chest at the foot of the bed and removed my basket.

"Is that not the same basket that you carried when you met Charles?"

"Yes, it is."

"Then why take it?"

"It carries the memories of my mother, and it reminds me that I... I..." I knew if I continued it would require an explanation Sarah would never understand.

"It reminds me of my mother."

"What happened to your mother?"

"It's a long story and we must hurry."

"Tell me as we hurry."

I paused. "You must tell no one," I said.

"Kathleen, you trusted me with your life. Now what does that tell you of our friendship?"

"Yes, I'm sorry. You have been more than a friend."

"Tell all and leave me with no more questions." Sarah smiled.

"My mother was a very gifted woman. In the small town in Scotland where I grew up, if you were in any way different you were labeled evil. My mother was accused of being someone sent to do harm, when all she wanted to do was to help people get well. There came a day when an elderly woman in our town became very ill, and every remedy given to her failed as her condition worsened. My mother offered to help, but the woman's husband forbade her. My mother knew if she didn't help the woman, she would soon die. When the woman's husband left for the day to plow in the field, my mother went into her home and fed her a special soup. The old woman's husband returned before my mother could leave, and he accused her of poisoning his wife. The people in the town valued this man's opinion and accused my mother of doing evil and... she was stoned to death. Two days later the woman my mother tended to had completely healed and she lived another seven years."

"That's dreadful, Kathleen. How old were you?"

"I was twelve."

"I'm so sorry. Kathleen?" Sarah paused. "You should keep this basket with you always to remind yourself that you are someone special, too."

"Come, now. We must keep moving," I said. Quickly Sarah and I gathered up the items she'd prepared. I took the clothes I had on and placed them back in the bed while Sarah poured kerosene throughout the house. Outside, I looked up at the window where I sat and wrote in my journal. I gazed across the path where I had envisioned our new home, filled with children, a garden filled with herbs, roots, and spices. I closed my eyes as tears streamed down my face.

"It's going to be okay, Kathleen, I promise you," said Sarah.

"Yes, I know. It's just so hard to believe that my life here is coming to an end."

"This is not an end. This is the path to your new beginning."

We hurried through the trees on our way to the wagon. The supplies were loaded. Everything was ready for my departure. Sarah and I waited in silence. A soft breeze rustled the leaves on the tall oaks and maples. From out of the bushes came a woman, her figure tall and slender. Her hair was long and black and tied at the ends with leather. Even in the waning light of dusk I could see her golden brown face as she approached. Above the rustling of the trees I could hear her already familiar faint cry. The woman approached me with a loving smile on her face that only a mother would understand, and she gently handed me my daughter.

"Beautiful child," the woman said to me.

"You know English?" I said.

"Yes, Sarah teach me."

"What is your name?"

"I am Savannah."

"What a beautiful name. What does it mean?"

"It means open plain."

"Thank you for caring for my daughter. I shall be forever grateful." I turned to Sarah. "I don't know how to thank you. You are my one and only friend in this new land, and I shall miss you dearly."

"You will make many new friends. But you must hurry. The sun is setting and I must return. Charles will be back soon from the mill to find that his wife has died in a horrible fire. Savannah knows the creek well, and after a day's journey it opens to a river. From there she will give you instructions on how to follow the river to the far south."

"Sarah, I will never forget you."

"I will never forget you, Kathleen."

I pressed my face close to hers. The streams of our tears mingled, became inseparable, just like our friendship. I boarded the wagon with my daughter and with Savannah as our guide on a journey to a place that I did not know. I held my child closely and thanked God we had escaped with our lives. I sensed she was going to be a special little girl, and I would do everything I could to make sure she discovered her life's journey.

Before me the sun was setting, and we would travel throughout the night. Behind me I could see in the far distance a bright orange glow, embers and smoke kissing the darkness. Everything I had known about Charles and my life with him would be reduced to mere ashes and dust. I felt no sympathy for Charles and how he would feel when he returned home, for the person I thought I had fallen in love with in fact never existed. For a brief moment I felt a heaviness weighing on my heart. But one look at my sweet daughter sleeping in my arms I realized that I was not alone, neither was I starting over. As Sarah said, I was embarking on a new beginning.

* * *

Annah stopped reading the journal and let out a deep sigh of relief. Her eyes widened as she anticipated what lie in wait for her on the next page. Except the remaining pages in the journal were blank, conveying only the fragrant aroma of spices. Carefully she turned back to the last words written. She was uneasy about why she felt so compelled to know more about someone she never met. But clarity came with but a word: *connection.* Kathleen Clarice O'Brien Hampton was alive inside of Annah, generations later. The very notion quieted Annah's thoughts, releasing a surge of emotions she could not verbalize.

She glanced at her watch. It was only 10:00 p.m. and she felt as if she had been living the life of Kathleen for years. She picked up the next journal, took a deep breath, adjusted the pillows behind her neck and back, and opened the journal of Savannah Grace Gladstone.

Now I can put to rest the question of where I received my birth name.

Chapter Seven

September 7, 1844

It has been three weeks since the funeral, and I still find myself meandering in the hallway outside my mother's bedroom in disbelief that she is actually gone. Today is no different. As I curl up in her bed and envelop my body in her white linen shawl, I can still smell the sweet fragrance of spices on her pillow mixed with a potpourri of assorted flowers lingering from the fragrance in her hair. I hugged her pillow as tight as I could, wishing I could lay my head in her lap just one more time to tell her how much I love her. I feel like a part of me has died with her. Everything she knew she taught me, and everything I need to become a woman she passed down to me through her life. She was indeed a woman of virtue, elegance, and determination. If I had only one wish, it would be that I had discovered a remedy that allowed her to live longer. I especially miss the times when we would sit in front of the fireplace and she would tell me the story over and over again of her life in Scotland before she met my father. The story would always conclude the same way, how her best friend Sarah helped her escape and how an Indian woman brought us all the way to Georgia from South Carolina.

I will forever remember her last words to me before she died. She said that I was different so that I could make a difference.

I closed my journal and laid my face on the soft pillows of my mother's bed. Tears streamed down my face, saturating the fibers. I buried my face even deeper, inhaling over and over her signature fragrance. I wanted to preserve it for an eternity. I was lost in the moment when I felt John's body come alongside mine. He wrapped his arms around my waist and pressed his face against my neck.

"I miss her so much, John."

"I know, Savannah. And you will continue to miss her. But you will also have something you can take with you that no one else has."

"What is that, my love?"

"The part of her that will never die--her knowledge and your memories."

"I have never experienced such pain. How am I supposed to get through this?"

"You will, one day at a time. And one day the sadness will be replaced with fond memories."

"Thank you for being here with me."

"I am your husband, and I would not have it any other way."

"John?" I whispered. "I know you love me, but since my mother died, I have been thinking about my own mortality."

"There is something more to this, isn't there?" He smiled.

"Yes, there is. It is twenty-eight years that we have been married. I'm forty-six years old, and chances are I may never have a baby. I don't want to deprive you of the joy of having a family. If you said to me right now you wanted to leave me and marry another, I would let you go."

John was silent. He knew me as a practical woman, not given to emotion, and I always meant what I said without regret. He took his arms from around me, slipped out of the bed, and got down on one knee.

"Madam? May I have your hand, please?" He caressed my hand as if he had been given a string of the finest pearls and kissed it gently.

"I have been suddenly released from my marriage without my consent and without a battle. Now that I am free I must admit I have admired you, dear madam, from afar for twenty-eight years. Your charm has captivated me. Your sincere love for people has impressed me. I don't care what your past may have been, nor do I care what your current status may be. It doesn't matter to me if you are able to bear for me ten children or none at all. I only have one desire, and one desire alone, and that is to spend the rest of my life loving you. Would you do me the honor of becoming Mrs. John Gladstone?"

I looked at John with adoring eyes.

"Sir, I'm sorry to report that I cannot accept your proposal. You see, I'm in love with a man who is exceptionally kind and loving, and he has promised to spend the rest of his life loving me."

"Then I will carry you away at this moment so he shall never find another love like yours."

John swept me off the bed and spun me around, the room filling with our laughter. He always had a way to make me laugh. It was one of the main reasons I fell in love with him. I was considered by many in our town to be a person who took life too seriously, and I was quite stoic until I met John. He is lighthearted, kind, and always had an optimistic outlook on life even when there appears to be no hope.

He swung me around again while kissing me on my neck, cheek, and then his mouth covered mine. Slowly he swayed me back and forth until I slipped from his arms and stood on my tiptoes with my arms around his neck, gently kissing his face.

"I love you, Mrs. Gladstone."

"I love you, too, Mr. Gladstone," I said.

"Now, I never, ever want to hear you say anything else about having children," John said, playfully scolding me. "Children will come when they come, and if they do not come, ours will still be full, happy lives."

"You're right. And I will be a good wife and not bring it up again," I said, hugging him.

"Besides, we have fifty-five acres of crop children that are in need of our attention."

"I will need to go to town and hire twice as many hands as we had last year."

"Savannah, you need to be very careful about the people you hire."

"John, I know what you are thinking, but I am determined to not take the slaves for granted like some of the plantation owners. I believe everyone should be treated with respect. I will gladly hire people of any color who want to earn an honest living."

"My love, people in town may think you to be an abolitionist." He smiled.

"My dear John, I *am* an abolitionist. I won't be threatened by anyone's gossip about my beliefs, and no one can tell me how to harvest our land. My mother brought me up to believe that no human should be owned by another."

"Sometimes I wonder where you get your liberal ideas."

"It is in my bloodline," I said, gently stroking John's strong chin.

"I just want us to be careful," John said. "There is a lot stirring. We may be leading up to a war if things don't change."

"Sometimes you have to fight for what you believe. If my mother didn't fight for our lives, I would not be having this conversation with you right now."

John shook his head. He knew I was opinionated and stubborn, just like my mother, and he respected me all the more for it.

"Before I go into town I will stop and visit Mrs. Dunbar. She is due any day now, and she has requested that I come personally and deliver her first child."

"You are becoming quite the preferred practitioner."

"Yes, I know. This will be the third child this month--four counting Mrs. Dunbar's slave, Adda, who is also due any day."

"You amaze me. You take care of our home, help harvest our land, and you're a midwife."

"I'm a doctor," I said with ease. "Midwife is a temporary label until the medical school realizes I am just as educated as any man."

John held me tightly. "How did I come to acquire such a wonderful gift? I cannot imagine my life without you, and I am grateful for your mother's wisdom to escape South Carolina."

I walked over to the side of the bed and picked up the basket that contained her journals. I could feel the sadness again filling my heart. I turned the pages and a familiar fragrance of spices and herbs filled my nostrils. My eyes overflowed with tears that fell onto the journal pages.

"John, this is all I have left of her."

"You have more than that, Savannah," he said, gently wiping the tears from my face. "You have her hair, her eyes, her beauty, and most of all her heart. And this will be a constant reminder to you that you are someone special, and special people have a gift to look beyond the normality of our existence and do the unexplainable. That is exactly what you have done with your life."

I dried the journal on my dress and placed it back in the basket. I walked over and sat at the window, where my mother would sit for hours and read and write in her journal. John sat next to me, the look in his eyes telling me what I needed to do. I looked around the room, which now contained boxes of my mother's clothing, shoes, and hats that I packed three days after the funeral.

"Are you ready to give them away?" John said.

"Yes," I sighed heavily.

"Then while you are in town, I will arrange for them to be transported to the slaves at the Wellington Plantation."

In the corner of the room stood a bookcase filled with every medical book imaginable. At three years old I could read basic literature, and by the time I was twelve, I had the ability to comprehend any medical book put before me.

"John? Please arrange for all of her books to be donated to the library."

"Savannah, no. You need them when you enter medical school."

"Why waste my time? Yesterday I received another rejection."

"You must try again, and again, and again."

"It is useless. A woman my age will never be accepted into medical school."

"Well, if they never accept you, you will go on record as the woman who made the most attempts to get into medical school." At that, John smiled and held me close as I took one last glance at the rooms surroundings. It was just three weeks ago she carried the sewing basket with her to the porch to sit and knit a scarf for the upcoming winter. The basket and all it held were the only things connecting me to a father I never knew. I remembered the first time I asked about him. I was three years old. I came into the kitchen, where my mother was preparing dinner, and out of the blue I asked her why we didn't have a man living in our home like the other children. She gave me a puzzled look, as she did whenever I offered something far beyond my young age. But she would always respond to me with truth and wisdom. She sat me on her lap and cradled me in her arms and said that a man who lives with a woman and their children is called Father. The parents of the children, who are the mother and father, should understand that children are a special gift given to both the parents. But sometimes one of the parents may not understand what to do with the gift, so instead of the gift going to waste, the gift is given to the parent who does understand.

"Your father did not understand, so you were given to me." She sealed her words with a kiss on my forehead, and I never asked about my father until the day I turned eight and my mother suggested I invite the children from school to come over. When I responded I would rather read than play with children, or dolls, she sat me down and told me about her life as a little girl and how she was different and did not have many friends. But what I will always remember her saying to me was that I was a child prodigy, and the world in which we lived may never understand why or how we are born the way we are, but I was born to make a difference, and I could not make a difference being alone.

"Something is heavy on your mind," John said.

"Yes. I was thinking about something my mother told me when I was about eight years old. That I'm supposed to make a difference."

"Yes, you are. That's why I think it would be good for you to try to get into medical school."

"I don't need medical school to make a difference. I am happy being with you, taking care of our home and the children and families in our town. I refuse to be judged by whether or not I wear britches or carry a black bag determine if I am qualified to become a doctor."

"Then, my dear, together we shall make a difference, with or without the medical schools' permission."

"I will get started with my first duty of the day by seeing Mrs. Dunbar, and I, Doctor, Mrs. John Markus Gladstone, will be home in time to cook your dinner."

"I love you, Dr. Mrs. Gladstone," John said, kissing me on my forehead. I smiled.

Chapter Eight

The Dunbar plantation was a breathtaking sight for anyone who traveled to Macon, Georgia. The two-story mansion was comparable to a small castle, with its 32 rooms decorated with the finest furniture, paintings, and rugs imported from around the world. The winding trail leading up to the mansion through a canopy of sprawling maple trees for at least a mile did not compare to the 5,000-acre plot that produced more than half the cotton in the county. The Dunbar family dynasty could be traced back to a prominent duke and duchess of England, and they spared no means to spread the fact they were descended from royalty. They entertained the wealthiest, dressed in the finest clothes, and threw the grandest ballroom parties, but with all of this grandeur, they were little respected by anyone outside their sphere of influence.

From Adda and Samuel's two-room cabin I could see Jonathan, the stable slave, preparing Mr. Dunbar's prize horse for a day of leisure riding. Jonathan meticulously brushed the tail of the animal and carefully picked clean the thick mane of any debris. He walked twice around the horse to ensure it would be as immaculately groomed as its owner. Samuel and Adda were field slaves, which meant they were given very little in terms of possessions and sustenance. Despite this their little cabin home was filled with warmth, love, and contentment, all of which was missing from the Dunbar mansion. The heels of my shoes easily dug into the dirt floor of the cabin. On one side of the room were two broken chairs held together by scraps of cloth. Next to the chairs, on a makeshift table, sat a small potted vase that housed a mixture of flowers and weeds. Across the room stew brewed in a black pot suspended over the fire in the fireplace. In the next room Samuel spoke to his wife, Adda, in a language unknown to me. The gentle tone of his voice led me to believe he was telling her everything was going to be all right for the arrival of their first child. It was the fifth day in a row I'd come to the Dunbar mansion to see how both Mrs. Dunbar and Adda were progressing in their pregnancies. I had presumed Mrs. Dunbar would have delivered by now, but it appeared Adda would precede her, so I decided this day to stay until both women had given birth.

I went into the room where Adda lay on a small bed made from leftover hay from the horse stable and scraps of cloth. She laid quite comfortably, with her husband, Samuel, close by holding her hand. They could not have been more than sixteen years of age.

"Do you think the child will come soon?" Samuel said in broken English.

"Yes, Samuel. Very soon," I said, smiling at the two of them.

"You are good to help me. I am afraid what will happen," Adda said, caressing her stomach.

"I want you to know everything is going to be fine."

"But you must check Massa's wife," Samuel said with concern.

"Don't worry about Mrs. Dunbar, Samuel. She's not going to deliver for a while now."

I looked into the eyes of the two African slaves, their hands and feet blistered and cut from long hours of picking cotton. But it had no effect on the countenance on their faces. Hope remained in their eyes, and it was a strength anyone who was not a slave could never fully understand. Samuel and Adda were among the first generation of slaves who learned to read and write, for buried underneath their makeshift bed they concealed books, secretly brought to them by children who thought it something of a private game to teach slaves to read and write.

A wave of weakness overcame me, and I grabbed Samuel's arm to steady my balance.

"Are you well?" Samuel said as he held me up.

"Yes, I-I'm fine. I haven't been my best for the past couple of days. But I'll be fine. It's probably just exhaustion."

"Do you eat?" said Adda.

"Actually, I haven't had much of an appetite, and when I do eat, I don't feel well."

Samuel and Adda smiled at each other. She looked over at me and pointed to my stomach and said something to Samuel in their native language. Samuel responded with a huge grin and they both laughed.

"What is it? Why are you laughing?"

"Nwa," said Adda, pointing at me again.

"She said in our native language, 'child.' You are with child," said Samuel.

"Yes. You are with child and you are here to bring our child into this new world," said Adda.

I placed my hand on my chest and could feel my heart racing. *This is not possible,* I said over and over in my mind. It was exactly 42 days from the last day of my discharge. *I thought my monthly flow was delayed because of the stress and worry over the death of my mother.*

"I couldn't possibly be having a child, not at this time in my life."

"In Nigeria, the place of our ancestors, we know every child has its time to come. Now is the time of your child."

"I have not paid any attention to what was going on with me. I've been preoccupied, and I have completely disregarded my symptoms."

"Now you know you are with child?"

"Yes, Adda, now I know. I'm going to have a baby! John and I are going to have a baby!"

I placed my hand on my stomach, and laughter came from within me like I have never experienced before.

"You are happy, yes?" said Samuel.

"Yes, I am very happy. I am overwhelmed with happiness." My thoughts immediately went to John. *He will be overjoyed when I tell him that we are finally going to have a baby.*

"My mother will not be here to share in our happiness," I said with longing.

"She will know. All who go before us wait on the high hills to hear the first cry of all who come after them."

"What a beautiful thought, Samuel. I will remember that when my child is born, but I must leave now and tell John."

"You leave us now?" Samuel said with concern.

"No worries, Samuel. I will not be long, just an hour's journey and I will return."

"Ahhhh!" Adda cried aloud.

"What is it, Adda? What are you feeling?"

"I do not know. The pain is more." She panted.

I felt Adda's stomach and discerned that her baby had already descended into the birth canal. When I checked her vaginally I knew her baby was in a breach position.

"Adda, try to breathe slowly."

Nwa! Nwa! Adda yelled, her hands clutching Samuel's arm.

"Samuel, I need your help. It is very important that Adda not push. Do you understand me? She must not push the baby out."

"Yes, yes, I understand."

"Now do whatever you can do to keep Adda focused. Hold her hands tight, have her look into your eyes, and tell her everything is going to be all right—just don't push."

Fear showed in Samuel's coal-black eyes. How could I tell a man that there was a 50/50 chance he would lose both his wife and his child? Adda groaned with the intensity of the pain that grew. She bit down into her bottom lip.

"Adda! No, no, just scream, let it out, let it out!" I said firmly. She shook her head and buried her teeth deeper. I tore pieces from the bottom of my undergarment and forced them into her mouth so that the cotton became a cushion between her teeth and her lip.

"Adda, listen to me. The child is in a difficult position. A position not for delivery. I will have to help you deliver your child, but you must pay close attention. You cannot push! Do you hear me? You must fight the feeling to push! Do you understand?"

Adda's eyes were as wide as those of a frightened horse. She nodded her head.

"Samuel, help her stay focused. Tell her to relax and to take deeper, longer breaths for me."

Adda responded as sweat dripped generously down her face and mingled with her tears.

"I know you are afraid, but it's going to be all right. By the time the sun sets you will have your baby in your arms."

Adda smiled and began taking deeper breaths.

In the distance I could faintly hear someone calling my name. When the voice grew closer, I could make out that it was Jonathan. Within seconds his heavy footsteps burst through the small cabin and into the room.

"Ms. Savannah, Mrs. Dunbar ready to have her baby. Mr. Dunbar say you come now."

I turned my head toward Adda and placed my hand on her stomach. There was no time.

"Tell Mr. Dunbar Adda is having her baby, and I will be there as soon as possible."

"But Ms. Savannah, Massa say you must come now!"

"Tell Mr. Dunbar he is not *my* master, and I will be there after I deliver Adda's child."

Jonathan stood frozen, his eyes glazed.

"Go, now!" I said.

Jonathan fled from the cabin, and his footsteps signaled he was well on his way back to the main house.

"Adda. It's time." I removed several items from the bag I brought with me for breech births. My experience as a midwife was that in repositioning the child the pain for the mother is so excruciating she rarely survives and the baby dies soon after. I prayed Adda and her child would not become another casualty.

"Adda, no, no! Do not push! Do not push!"

* * *

From the front porch of Samuel and Adda's tiny cabin I could make out in the darkness the shadows of three horses approaching. Before Mr. Dunbar arrived I could already sense the anger and hatred he was prepared to unleash upon me. I, on the other hand, was prepared for whatever the consequences. My restitution was that a child was born tonight, and the father was very happy to have both his wife and son alive. The horses drew closer. I could see the two other gentlemen riding with Mr. Dunbar, the sheriff and his deputy.

"There she is!" yelled Mr. Dunbar. "She is the one responsible for this atrocious event."

The horses simultaneously stopped in front of the cabin. Mr. Dunbar dismounted his horse in a fury. "Arrest this woman immediately!" he shouted.

The deputy stepped forward and spat a deep, dark brown liquid from his mouth onto the front porch of the cabin.

"Is this your darkie's cabin?" he said, wiping his mouth on his shirtsleeve.

I remained silent, looking into the faces and reading their guilty verdict already announced on my life. I walked over to the edge of the porch and looked straight into the eyes of the deputy.

"This is the home of Samuel and Adda."

The sheriff stepped forward and put up his hand to silence Mr. Dunbar and the deputy's perverse profanities aimed at me.

"Mrs. Gladstone? I need you to answer me just one question," the sheriff said, tilting his hat upward.

"I will answer anything you request."

"Were you present in the room of Mrs. Olivia Dunbar when she gave birth to a baby boy this evening?"

"No, sir, I was not present."

"Then Mr. Dunbar, I cannot arrest this woman. She was not present when your wife gave birth to your dead son."

"You must arrest her! If she had come when I demanded, my son would be alive. Instead she refused and helped these darkies! I demand you arrest her now!"

"Mr. Dunbar, I'm sorry for your loss, but you have given no cause for this woman to be arrested."

"What about my rights!"

"What rights are you referring to, Mr. Dunbar?" I said, taking another step forward.

"My rights as a law-abiding citizen of Macon County. My rights that the Dunbar family name takes precedence above the law."

Mr. Dunbar walked toward the cabin, and I stepped in front to block him from entering the door.

"Move out of my way," he sneered, raising his hand threateningly.

"Mr. Dunbar?" the sheriff said, grabbing his arm. "It has been a long night, and I think it best that you tend to comforting your wife and grieving family."

"What about my rights? I demand that justice be served tonight against this woman and others like her who dare to follow in her footsteps!"

"Mr. Dunbar! As the sheriff of this county, it is my view the matter is settled."

Mr. Dunbar leaned toward me. His bloodshot eyes displayed a hatred I had never seen before.

"You will suffer for my loss," Mr. Dunbar said, spitting on my shoes. "You and those no good n..."

"Sheriff? Annah interrupted. Given the circumstances, I would like to purchase Samuel and Adda from Mr. Dunbar. You, Mr. Dunbar, may name your price."

"Five thousand dollars. Each." He glared.

"You will have the money in the morning."

In silence Mr. Dunbar mounted his horse and rode fiercely back to the main house.

"See to it that Mr. Dunbar gets home tonight," the sheriff said to his deputy.

"Yes, sir," the deputy said, spitting more of the dark liquid from his mouth, soiling the hem of my dress.

The deputy headed toward the Dunbar house, leaving the sheriff and I alone. I was intrigued by his response to Mr. Dunbar. I knew the sheriff to be an upright man of the law, but I also knew Mr. Dunbar had a great deal of influence in government affairs. He had one ulterior motive: to get what he wanted through manipulation, bribery, and threats. I was sorry for his loss, but not for the decision I made to help Adda.

"Mrs. Gladstone, what you did in helping the slaves will not be favorably received by the people here. You and your mother have always been respected for your work. But you need to be careful helping the slaves. Help them, but be careful how you do it."

"I would be careful, too, sheriff," I said. "You may be perceived to be an abolitionist."

The sheriff smiled, tilted his hat forward, mounted his horse, and swiftly rode away.

Samuel helped me prepare Adda and their son for the ride back home. We left everything in the cabin as it was. I did not want them to have any reminders of the Dunbar plantation. I watched Samuel hold his newly born son as Adda rested quietly in the back of the carriage. I anticipated telling John we would finally be parents. It brought me a certain peace, and the events of the Dunbar plantation vanished as the road leading to the main mansion disappeared in the night. The path to our home was long and dark, but from a distance I could see light not too far off. I presumed it to be the approaching dawn until we passed through the meadow, where I saw a horrific sight. Our land was completely engulfed in flames.

"Samuel!" I said. "Unhook one of the horses. I will ride to the house and you can bring Adda." Within moments I was riding as fast as I could. By the time I arrived several families were there with buckets of water in an attempt to put out the fire enveloping our home.

"John! John!"

"Ms. Savannah," yelled one of the neighbors. "He ran back inside the house saying he had to save something."

"John!" I cried out. I ran toward the house, but the heat from the flames held me back. Bursts of flames shot high into the air. I put my hand over my face and tried to run into the house when a hand grabbed me and pulled me back.

"Let me go! I've got to find John!" I struggled, but it was no use.

"Ms. Savannah, I can't let you go in there," said Samuel.

"I've got to save him!" I sobbed.

"No, Ms. Savannah, you have *nwa*." I turned, and behind Samuel I could see Adda sitting in the carriage holding the baby. I ceased my struggle. I placed my hands upon my stomach and remembered that, much like my mother saved my life, I needed to save the life of my child. I turned away from the fire and walked slowly toward the carriage, which seemed to me miles away. The grief I felt for my mother's death and the loss of John overwhelmed me. My legs felt as if weighted down by large rocks and soon gave out. Samuel carried me the distance to the carriage. My eyes squeezed shut and my head pounded with pain over my loss. Behind me I could hear the crackling sound of my home ablaze, and within seconds it collapsed, sending flames shooting even higher into the air, lighting up the sky for miles. I took in a deep breath and inhaled the fragrance of my roots and spices burning in the acreage next to our home. Our entire harvest and home was gone. Tears mixed with soot streamed down my face and into my mouth—the taste as bitter as my loss.

Samuel placed me in the back of the carriage next to Adda. I laid my head on her chest and cried uncontrollably. Samuel hitched my horse back to the carriage and led us away from the house. All was lost--my home, my husband, and the precious fields where my mother had spent most of her life planting. One by one the remaining neighbors left holding empty water buckets, and soon the house and field were in the distance, embers of orange light glowing in the dark.

"Ms. Savannah, you are a strong woman. You will plant again," said Adda.

* * *

I turned over on my side, the movement sending aches of anguish through my entire body. The night's events left me utterly depleted. I remembered that we rode for about an hour until we came to the home of George and Rebecca Keffler. They graciously took us in, in part because I had delivered all seven of their children. I took in a deep breath and my nostrils filled with an all-too-familiar fragrance. I thought perhaps it was my dress that carried the fragrance of the roots and spices, but I had removed it before washing and getting into bed. The fragrance aroused my curiosity.

"John!" I leaped from the bed, throwing my arms around his neck and smothering him with kisses. "You're alive! You're alive. Thank God, you are alive!"

"Savannah, Savannah," he replied, returning my enthusiastic kisses.

I could hardly catch my breath as tears poured from my eyes.

"I thought I had lost you," he said.

"I thought I had lost you, too. One of the neighbors said you went into the house to get something. I tried to go after you, but the house was…"

"I did go back in. I knew that if I could save only one thing it was your mother's journals."

"Oh, John, it was foolish of you to risk your life for that."

"Once I got the basket there was no other way out but through the back of the house. I barely made it out when I saw the barn was on fire. I set the animals free and decided to ride to the Dunbar Plantation to find you."

"Something terrible happened tonight."

"I know. I came across the sheriff and his deputy, and he told me what occurred."

"It wasn't my fault Mr. Dunbar's child died."

"I know. I also know that Mr. Dunbar is responsible for our loss, and I am going to find a way to get back at him for what he has done."

"I don't care about what Mr. Dunbar did. I only care that you are alive."

"Savannah, we must see that he is brought to justice."

I picked up the basket and breathed in the fragrance. I took out the journal inside and placed it on my stomach.

"Are you all right?"

"Yes, I am," I said softly. "I want to leave Macon."

"You have lived here your entire life. Why would you want to leave?"

"Because I want to raise our child in a place where it will not be affected by happened here."

"Child?" John stuttered. "Did you say child?"

"Yes, we are having a baby!"

"I'm going to be a father?"

"Yes, you are!" I took John's hand and placed it on top of my mother's journal, which rested on my stomach. We looked into each other's eyes. Our long-awaited prayer had been answered.

* * *

Annah turned several pages of the journal, only to find them empty. She was curious as to why it ended so abruptly and concluded that perhaps her four times great-grandmother Savannah Gladstone had written more of her life in the last remaining journal. It was 12:15 a.m. Annah picked up the journal, repositioned herself on the cushions, and opened it—only to find something that completely surprised her.

Chapter Nine

August 8, 1930

I suppose the sensible way to begin this journal is to properly introduce myself to whomever happens upon this document and finds themselves compelled to read the accounts of my life, and those of my dear progenitors. My name is Frances Allen Harper, after the renowned poet, and I am approximately 40 years old. If you are wondering why the ambiguity surrounding my actual birth date, it is because no one really knows when I was born. I was told that as an infant I was placed in an old sewing basket and left on the steps of the Weatherford Orphanage in Baltimore, Maryland, in the winter of 1890. The school maid happened to hear a baby crying, and when she opened the front door of the orphanage, she saw an old woman hurrying away. There was no note as to who the old woman was, nor any information as to why I was abandoned. Also, I had no name. The only things left alongside me in the sewing basket were two journals authored by one woman named Savannah and the other, her mother Kathleen. I read the journals for the first time when I was eight years old then locked them away. Foolishly thinking that would change my perspective about its contents or that I was an orphan. However as I grew older, the desire to read them again passed with time. And the old saying that time heals all wounds is assuredly a myth to those who have never experienced pain. Therefore, I spent my entire life behind the walls of the Weatherford Orphanage, hoping one day to be adopted. But as I approached the age of 12, each day I would let go of the dream of ever becoming part of a family. Since the day Weatherford opened its doors to abandoned children, I am the only orphan to have never left its four walls. I have come to know rejection and abandonment all too well. They have become synonymous with love and affection. My only solace was the fact that I had a roof over my head, hot meals every day, and a library of books to read; I pretty much have had the basic necessities of life, so what more could I want. At 21 years of age, I was hired on as a schoolteacher for the younger children. It's odd sometimes to sleep in one room and wake up and get dressed and walk down a flight of stairs to work. I never once thought to find out about my parents, and certainly after all these years it did not matter to me what became of them. I felt because they abandoned me as an infant, they must be horrible people and I had no desire to know them. But today, everything about my life--who I am, and what is to become of me--is going to change. Four weeks ago I received a strange package in the mail. It has completely changed my life, and it is where my journey begins, today.

I returned the journal back to the sewing basket and exhaled. I felt nervous, anxious, and scared. The empty entrance halls of Weatherford echoed the silence of my life lived here. I could have never imagined that I would be leaving, but the day had arrived. I watched as Mrs.

Wentworth approached me with arms outstretched and tears overflowing her round pink face.

"Frances, I don't know how we are going to survive while you are gone."

"The school will do just fine."

"Did you pack everything you need?"

"Yes, practically everything I own can fit into my suitcase."

"Promise me you will call as soon as you arrive?"

"I will."

"The children are going to miss you terribly."

"I will miss them, too."

Mrs. Wentworth held on to me as if she would never see me again. I completely understood her affection. She had been like a mother to me since the very beginning. Because I had no parents of my own, she took it upon herself to take care of me, as she and her husband of 50 years could not have any children of their own. She believed that one day I would become the headmistress of the school and eventually take over the orphanage when she and Mr. Wentworth could no longer manage its affairs. I was honored that she would want me to take over on her behalf. But I didn't know if this was something that I wanted.

"Mrs. Wentworth, should I decide not to return, I want to thank you for everything you have done for me. I will never forget you or Weatherford. You both shall always remain in my heart."

"You speak as if you have already made up your mind that you are not going to return. Please say you are coming back?"

"I don't know how to answer that. I don't know what I will find or where my findings may lead me. I just know that if I don't leave now I may regret this for the rest of my life."

I could see a sort of comfort in Mrs. Wentworth's eyes. An assurance that I had made the right decision, and that it was time for me to leave and find the answers to all my life's questions she could no longer answer.

"Promise me then that you will come back, to properly say goodbye?"

"I promise."

"I hope you find what you are looking for, Frances, and I wish you God's best."

"Thank you, Mrs. Wentworth." I stood back and took one last look around the halls of the orphanage. I hugged and kissed Mrs. Wentworth one last time before pushing open the large doors leading to the front courtyard. The cabdriver stood outside the cab waiting impatiently. He tilted his hat, grabbed my bags, and placed them in the back of the taxi. As we drove off, I forced myself not to look back as tears streamed down my cheeks. Everything I knew was now behind me.

The taxicab driver drove through the heart of town to the train station. It had been ten years since I ventured out to the city. I spent most of my leisure time tutoring students on the weekends, and any other spare time I spent in the orphanage library. Mrs. Wentworth discovered that at the age of two I could read at a sixth grade level, so she was constantly purchasing new books to keep up with my precocious skills. When I was ten, she allowed me to volunteer as the librarian in the afternoons. By my standards, Weatherford's library was comparable to that of any small university library.

With the sewing basket next to me on the seat, I retrieved the package I had received in the mail four weeks prior, examining the outside as if I were seeing it for the first time. I studied the postmark indicating the package originated in Atlanta, Georgia, but there was no return address. I slowly withdrew the item directing my quest, a small dark brown glass bottle about four inches long with a corked top. I ran my fingers across the embossed words, "S.G. Gladstone – Cough Formula." Clearly there was a connection to the bottle and the journal authored by Savannah Grace Gladstone. I could not help but wonder how I might possibly be connected with the bottle, the journals, and the sewing basket. Perhaps the bottle was sent by the person who abandoned me, or a lost relative, or even someone reaching out for help. Maybe there was a dark past or family secret, and the bottle was a clue that could lead me on an adventure or perhaps even my own demise. My mind filled with possibilities. *It's too late to turn back now*, I resolved. Atlanta was a three-day train ride from Baltimore. I would have plenty of time to re-read the two journals and write in my journal the events that took place. There was a reason why Savannah and Kathleen were compelled to set down the details of their lives in words. There was a reason why someone undisclosed had sent me a bottle. Whoever these women were, something phenomenal must have occurred in order to account for me being left on the steps of an orphanage. Otherwise, why didn't this woman just let me die?

The taxi pulled into Baltimore's train station. Through the crowds of people I managed to find my cabin in the coach section of the train and was relieved to finally relax after the long ride. I positioned my belongings in the above compartment and sat down to write in my journal. I was anxious to get under way in searching for the answers to questions that had haunted me since I first received the mysterious bottle. I tried to focus my thoughts on writing, but the impending journey caused my palms to sweat, and the pen I held slipped from my hand. I reached down to pick it up, only to find my hand meeting the hand of a stranger.

"Excuse me, but I presume this is yours," the gentleman said, handing the pen to me.

"Yes, it is. Thank you."

"My pleasure," he said, hovering.

"Is there something else, sir?"

"Yes, there is. I believe you are sitting in my seat," he said, showing me his train ticket.

"I'm terribly sorry. Let me gather my things and I'll move immediately." When I stood up I noticed he looked to be in his late forties. His hazel green eyes were directly at the same level as mine. This was unusual because I was just shy of six feet. By the way he dressed, I judged he was someone of stature. His charcoal-gray tweed suit complemented the silver tie that matched his salt-and-pepper hair. His smile was warm and his voice friendly.

"You can stay," he said, returning my bags to the compartment.

"It's quite all right. I don't mind moving."

"Actually, there is no need for you to move. There is plenty of room for the both of us."

"But you said I was in your seat."

"That's true. You are in my seat, and the seat across from you is mine also."

"Are you expecting someone?"

"Quite the contrary. I routinely purchase two train tickets so I don't have to sit next to people who talk too much, or haven't bathed in days. In your case, it is reserved for a beautiful woman who I can engage in a stimulating conversation."

"Sir, I could very well be boring and not the slightest bit interested in stimulating your intellect."

"Well now, that is not at all possible."

"What makes you so sure?"

"You have a journal, so I have concluded you are either a journalist or a poet. Both I find most intriguing."

"You are quite presumptuous, sir. But I don't know you, so I'll just go to my assigned seat."

"Before you leave, let me introduce myself. I'm Franklin Bradshaw, and it is a pleasure to meet you, Miss…?"

"Frances. My name is Frances."

"Frances. Frances who?"

"Just Frances."

"It's a pleasure to meet you, Just Frances. Now that we have been properly introduced, would you be so kind as to engage me in idle banter?"

His demeanor was comforting, and I was intrigued by his attentiveness and intelligence.

"My name is Frances Harper." I smiled and extended my hand to shake his, but my hand was awkwardly met with his gentle kiss on the back of my hand. Interesting. I never had a man kiss my lips, let alone my hand.

"Again, the pleasure is all mine, Frances Harper." He smiled and took a seat across from me. I did not know what to make of his personality. He was obviously forward and assertive, yet humbly reassuring.

"Well, now that we are past the awkward introductions, tell me about yourself, Frances."

"There is nothing to tell."

"Come now, we have at least three days to get to know each other. Don't be shy."

"Honestly, there is nothing to tell because… because I don't know." My stoic expression spoke more than a thousand words. I turned to look out the window. The train had just begun its exit from the station.

For a moment Franklin said nothing, until his response totally caught me off guard. "I hope you do find what you are looking for." He spoke softly.

"How do you know I'm on a quest?"

"When you pulled your bag from the compartment, I noticed on the label the name Weatherford Orphanage. Is that where you are from?"

"Yes, it is."

"And what is your quest, if I may ask?"

The words seemed to be trapped in my throat. Here I was, sitting with a complete stranger, sharing with him a part of my life I knew nothing about. But I finally said the words that had been locked inside of me for years.

"I'm on a quest to find my mother."

"And she is at what point of destination?"

"Atlanta, Georgia, I presume. I received a package in the mail about four weeks ago, giving me a clue as to where I should start. I may not find anything when I get there, but I want to at least make an attempt."

"Where will you start once you get there?"

"Probably the hall of records to see if there is a birth certificate on a Savannah Gladstone."

"Savannah? Is it your mother's name?"

"I'm not sure who she is, but she is definitely a clue."

"How so?" Franklin sat forward in his seat as if listening to a story from a mystery novel. I reached into the sewing basket and retrieved the package that contained the glass bottle.

"This is the clue." Franklin took the brown bottle in his hand and examined it as if it were fine china. "Is the bottle familiar to you?" I said.

"Not really, but I would say that this bottle is well over seventy-five years old."

"You're a doctor?"

"Not quite. I studied pharmaceutical medicine in college and decided that I didn't want to spend the next eight to ten years studying to become a doctor, so I changed my profession."

"What is your occupation?"

"I teach pharmacology at a private university in Atlanta." We both smiled at the irony.

"What are you doing in Baltimore?"

"I travel to Baltimore about four times a year to attend seminars so I can keep abreast of the latest information in my field," he said, looking the bottle over several times.

"Frances, you have found a piece of your past that could possibly lead to who you are and where you came from. Tell me, how long have you been at Weatherford Orphanage?"

"I've been there since... since I was an infant."

"Why didn't you leave before you received this mysterious bottle?"

"I-I... why are you asking me these questions?"

"Because it appears that you have never asked yourself these questions. Otherwise you would have left the orphanage long before you received this bottle."

Franklin's words unsealed the door to my heart for the first time in years. I wanted to excuse myself from his presence so he would not see the tears filling my eyes. Instead I sat frozen. One by one tears ran down my face, but I didn't care. I found solitude in the truth. Franklin removed a handkerchief from his suit pocket. I expected any moment he would hand it to me, but instead he returned the handkerchief to his pocket and said the unexpected.

"Let the tears fall. Apparently they are long overdue."

Chapter Ten

The train ride to Atlanta was long and yet invigorating. I paid little attention to any of the outside scenery, mainly because Franklin and I seemed to be engaged in nonstop conversations from the time we left Baltimore. He is an extraordinary man, and I am intrigued by his life and the stories he has to tell of all the places he has traveled. When I spoke of my menial adventures at the orphanage, he seemed equally taken with stories about the children. There was one moment when he displayed signs of emotion. Sadly it was the story of how he lost his wife to one of his closest friends. He said there was implication throughout the five years of their marriage that she had engaged in an extramarital affair. However, he chose to deny it for years, until early one summer morning while having breakfast she said to him that she did not love him as a wife should love her husband. She packed her bags and left. Within a year, he received word through a mutual friend that his ex-wife and former best friend were married. That was ten years ago, and since then he had been predisposed with work and traveling. He concluded from that single heartbreak that falling in love just wasn't worth the pain. I envied his pain.

* * *

Five days ago I arrived in Atlanta. I know now that meeting Franklin on the train was no happenstance. He has been kind enough to help me with my search to find my biological mother. His knowledge of the court system and county records has been instrumental, although as yet I have found no information on a Savannah Grace Gladstone. One thing I do know is I have enjoyed his company so much that I have been completely distracted from writing in my journal. Our days have been spent at the public library, the hall of records, and the chamber of commerce, searching through pages and pages of records. In the evenings Franklin insisted that we tour the historical sites of the city, given that I have never really ventured outside of Weatherford. And personally I think he takes pleasure seeing the variety of expressions that parade across my face when I sample various foods for the very first time. I find myself partial to chicken that has been prepared in a skillet and smothered in a delicious dark sauce known in the South as country gravy. Accompanying the smothered chicken is a corn bread covered in a green liquid called pot liqueur. Southerners do have a way with cooking as well as with their words. I've grown rather fond of both.

I placed the journal in my satchel as I waited patiently in the lobby of the Atlanta Gardens Hotel for Franklin. Today would be the last time he could spend time to help me with my search. Classes at the university would begin soon, and Franklin needed to turn his focus toward teaching. I didn't expect him to help me at all, but I was so grateful that he had.

Through the glass doors of the hotel entrance I could see Franklin's tall, well-proportioned frame. It had never dawned on me until now that Franklin was a handsome gentleman. He walked with confidence, attracting the attention of any woman who passed him by, although for some reason his eyes stayed focused on me.

"Good morning, Frances."

"Good morning, Franklin." We would greet each other precisely the same way each morning, except this time he took my hand and placed it on his arm as we walked out of the hotel toward his car. I heard him saying words, but my mind concentrated on one action, Franklin's hand touching mine.

"...would you agree it would be a practical start?" Franklin stopped beside me. "Frances, you haven't heard a word I have said to you."

"I'm sorry, I was slightly distracted. Please tell me again."

"In one of the journals you said there was a slave named Adda. Maybe we have been searching in the wrong manner and should be looking for Adda and Samuel instead of Savannah Gladstone."

"Yes, yes of course. That never occurred to me."

"You know, my dear Watson, after five days of searching we have come up with absolutely nothing. You and I would make lousy detectives." He laughed, and it was the first time that I could remember hearing myself laugh.

We drove back to the courthouse. Not far down on the list of names we came across the name and address of a Samuel, Adda, and Eddington Smith.

"Well my dear Watson, I think we've found ourselves a grand clue," Franklin said in a muddled British accent.

"Indeed," I mimicked.

"We'd better get going. According to the address, we have a long drive ahead of us."

Franklin and I said nothing during the entire drive, which was an unusual twist given we talked nonstop on the train from Baltimore. The silence reflected our preoccupation with the fact we had finally found something, and each mile brought me closer to what Savannah Gladstone wrote in her journal. No longer fiction, it was factual and soon to become a reality.

The countryside of Atlanta was a quiet sanctuary of beautifully landscaped homes nestled between green hills and majestic trees and pastures that seemed to extend for miles. The air was lighter than the thick, muggy city air I breathed, and I relished taking in long, deep breaths.

"Are you nervous?" Franklin said, breaking the silence.

"Yes, a little. But mostly I'm feeling anxious. I want to hurry up and get this over with."

Fifteen minutes later we arrived at the address we had for the Smiths. It was a modest one-story house sitting on an acre or more of land. The yard was immaculate and on the porch sat four rocking chairs. Franklin pulled into the empty driveway, and my heart slowed and pounded hard in my chest. I held the glass bottle in my hand, unconsciously rubbing the initials of S.G. Gladstone as if it were a magic lamp. Franklin opened my door and extended his hand to help me out of the car.

"Are you okay?" Franklin said, waiting for me to take his hand.

"I can't do this. I've changed my mind."

"You have come too far. You can't turn away now."

"I'm not prepared for this."

"Frances, you're afraid and it's expected."

"No, it's not that."

Franklin knelt next to me, staring. "Talk to me," he said.

"I've spent my whole life at Weatherford, angry and purposely avoiding the day I would meet my birth mother."

"Why?"

"I'm afraid of the other possible truth. That perhaps my mother abandoned me out of nothing nefarious, but because she was trying to protect me, and I have wasted a lifetime hating her for the wrong reason."

"You will never find out the truth sitting in the car."

"What am I supposed to say to her after all these years? How should I address her? What was my given birth name? Why did she abandon me? Do I have siblings? Do I--"

"Frances, Frances, stop," Franklin interrupted, placing his fingers on my lips. "You are getting ahead of yourself. Now, take a deep breath and relax. You don't know what you will find when you knock on the door. Let's just take it one step at a time."

"You're right. I'm just nervous and anxious. Please forgive my outburst."

"At this point, you are entitled to feel whatever emotions surface. Frances, you are an amazing woman inside and out, and I guarantee you that whoever the Smiths are, or whatever role they played in the life of your family, they will find you just as exceptional as I do."

Franklin took my hand, leading me up to the front door of the house. My palms sweat. I tried to withdraw my hand from his out of embarrassment. He only held it tighter. "No worries," he said reassuringly.

"They're all gone," said a voice from behind. I turned around to see a young Negro boy about ten years of age sitting on a bicycle with a fishing pole in his hand.

"Hello, young man," Franklin said.

"If you are looking for the Smiths, they're gone."

"Gone where?" I said.

"Back to Macon, Georgia. They left about a week ago and said they did not know when they would be back."

"Do you know why they left?"

"Little Georgie told me his great-grandmother was dying and it was her wish to be buried in Macon, so the family packed up and left. Are you two going to be our new neighbors? I hope you have kids so I can have someone to go fishing with."

"No, we're not moving in. We're just looking for the Smiths," said Franklin. "Can you tell us the name of his great-grandmother?"

"You should know that if you've been around here long enough. Everybody knows Ms. Adda Smith."

"Thank you, young man. You have been extremely helpful." Franklin handed the little boy some change, and he rode off on his bike.

"Frances, I think we need to get started if we are going to get to Macon by evening."

"Franklin, wait. I am so grateful for all your help, but I can't allow you to continue to do this. You have other priorities, and I've taken far too much of your time already."

"This is my priority. Besides, my dear Watson, we shall not give up until this mystery has been solved to your satisfaction."

The hour-and-a-half drive to Macon was different. We chattered the entire time. Franklin shared with me about his life as a child in Kansas City, Missouri. He was the eldest of nine children, and there were times when he had to be father and brother to his siblings, who eventually ended up hating him. He said he didn't care how they felt about him. He forced his siblings to do things for their own good. Now I realized why he was so obstinate. Franklin had a quiet type of strength. He knew what he wanted and where he was going, and it was a quality I found admirable. In all my years at Weatherford I had never trusted in anyone enough to share my deepest secret. I felt I could trust Franklin, even with a secret I'd told no one outside of Weatherford. And regardless of how Franklin would react, after I find my mother we would probably never see each other again. I hoped I was wrong.

"I have been talking non-stop for some time now. Say something, please," said Franklin.

"I don't have much to say."

"Then tell me another story about the orphanage."

"There are no more stories. At least none that have a happy ending."

"Tell me. I don't care if it is sad. They are your stories."

"All right, but I will only tell you the ending of the story."

"Why not the whole story?"

"Because I don't know the beginning, the middle is too painful, and the end, I fear, is going to be just like the beginning."

Franklin took my hand and held it for the remainder of the drive.

We reached the Macon County Records Office just before closing and were able to get the address of Adda Smith. Unlike the neighborhood in Atlanta, Adda's home was located in the poorest area. I assumed the neighborhood was still experiencing the effects of the Depression, and it was clear the people there had become comfortable with poverty. The houses were small, rundown shacks aligned in a row. Many of them had no windows or plywood was applied to places where windows were missing. The adults and the elderly sat on the porch steps in the heat of the evening smoking a cigarette or whittling with a knife while fanning flies that seemed to blend in with their dark skin. The children who played seemed oblivious to the surrounding conditions. Some had on the barest necessities of clothing. Many of the younger children played barefooted, the red clay dirt molding to their feet like socks.

"Are you ready?" Franklin said as he stopped in front of the house.

"I suppose there is no turning back now."

"After today is over you will probably have only one regret."

"What is that?"

"That you should have done this sooner."

From the moment we stepped out of the car, the eyes of everyone watched us walk through the dirt and up the wooden steps. Before I had a chance to knock I could see through the screen door the figure of a tall, elderly gentleman.

"May I help you?" he said in a heavy voice.

"Is this the home of Adda Smith?"

The man behind the screen door paused then pushed it open. "Come in. There isn't much time left, so you should make your peace quickly," he urged. He motioned for us to follow him through the narrow living room, through the kitchen, and to a small room that was an addition onto the back of the house.

"When you go in, there is no need to explain what you did. The past is the past and she understands. Just ask her to forgive you, and nothing else needs to be said." The gentleman took out a handkerchief from his pocket and wiped his eyes. "We don't expect her to be with us much longer."

I looked at Franklin, puzzled. It was clear a number of white folks had treated Adda inappropriately, and they needed to make sure they made amends before she passed. The elderly gentleman stepped back to allow us to enter the small bedroom. The room was illuminated with several burning candles and void of décor. In the room's only window sat an electric fan to help vent the heat. Two middle-aged negro women sat in the opposite end of the bedroom, one with her eyes closed and her arms folded around her waist, rocking back and forth. She softly hummed a song while the other woman comforted her by gently rubbing her back and shoulders. In the center of the room was an old iron-framed twin bed just large enough to hold the small, frail body of Adda Smith. Her head rested on white pillows, and the embroidered comforter covering her body was decorated with intricate symbols, colors, and drawings from her African heritage. Franklin let go of my hand as I slowly walked over and sat in the chair beside the bed. My mind was completely blank. I could not find the

words to speak. The subtle creak in the chair moved Adda
to turn her head toward me, and in a soft, shallow whisper
she spoke.

"It's okay, child," she said, stretching her withered
hand to me. I took her hand in mine and slowly helped her
raise it to my face. "Come closer, child." With her hand
in mine, Adda gently touched every part of my face as if
she were tracing the route of someplace familiar to her
touch. She placed my hand upon her frail chest and said,
"The beauty in your face is the same as your grandmother,
Savannah."

Tears poured and I cried uncontrollably as she drew me
near to lay my face upon her chest.

"You have come a long way, Frances. You need not weep
anymore," she said, stroking my hair.

"How do you know my name?"

"I know everything about you, child."

"Then I have not journeyed in vain?"

"No, you have come just as I thought you would. Now
ask, just ask… I still have time to answer."

"Please, tell me, are you the woman who left me on the
steps of the Weatherford Orphanage?" I said, sitting up with
Adda's hand cupped in mine.

"It was December 1, 1890, and you were exactly three
weeks old."

"Three weeks old?"

"Yes."

"And are you the one who sent me the package in the
mail?"

"Yes, my child."

"Then you know where I may find my mother?"

"It is not your mother you are looking for."

"I made this journey to find her."

"No, Frances. You made this journey to find who you are." Adda took a deep breath and turned to the woman sitting in the chair, who immediately responded. She took the pillows that rested underneath Adda's head and propped them up so Adda could breathe more easily.

"You have traveled here only to find truth."

"I only know one truth. I was abandoned by my mother."

"It is the truth, but it is not the answer… Her name is Emily."

"Emily," I repeated softly. "Is she still alive?"

"No, she is not. No one knows exactly where she died, but I do know it was not on this soil."

"Tell me, please, all that you know of her life."

"I was there when your grandmother, Savannah, gave birth to her. She was a beautiful child, and your parents were happy and blessed to have her at such a time in their lives. Emily was different from all the other children her age. She was very smart, and your grandparents had the best of plans for her life, to follow in the footsteps of your family's heritage. But when she was sixteen, Emily changed. She had a different heart than your mother and father, and she fell in love with an elderly man, three times her age. Your grandparents did not approve of this man or the relationship. His face was white like the snow, but his heart was dark and ugly. His words were filled with deception, and Emily was too young to see the truth. This dark man married your mother and took her across the ocean to another land. A place no one knew. Your grandmother would receive letters from her. She would write saying all was well. No matter where Emily laid her head in this faraway place, your grandmother knew that all was not well. Years went by, and then suddenly the letters stopped. Your grandparents searched for her for many years, but their money and old age would not permit them to continue."

I hung on Adda's every word. My heartbeat could not keep up with the pounding of every new detail she revealed about my mother. I held her hand, hoping that in between her deep breaths she would not slip away.

"Did my grandparents have any more children?"

"Emily was their only child." Adda's breathing became shallow. The women in the corner came to her side to offer her water, but Adda refused. "Let me be," were her only words to the women, who retreated back to their spots.

"Years after your grandparents passed, Emily came to me, here in this very house. She was small. She had no life in her body except one. You were her only hope. She told me to never tell a soul she had come to me for help. I hid Emily in this room, the place where you were born. And one day I rose early and heard you crying. I came into the room and Emily was gone. She left me money and a note that said for me to take you to a place far away where no one would ever find you."

"How could she just leave me with no name, no family, no connection?"

"During your birth, I saw them," Adda said, her breathing increasingly shallow. "Bruises and scars on her body where she had been beaten for years, for the man she married had many wives whom he hurt badly. Your mother vowed that your father would never find you and make you suffer like she and the other women suffered."

Adda struggled to breathe. She took my hand and laid it upon her chest. "Your mother loved you, and she had to do what was right." Adda coughed again and again. The women who sat at the foot of the bed this time watched without offering any assistance. Adda squeezed my hand with what little strength remained in her.

"Now you know where you come from." Adda's voice changed to a whisper. "Rest in who you are to become. I can say no more. I must rest."

I took Adda's hand and pressed my lips into her palm.

"Thank you for saving my life," I said with tears flowing.

The woman who sat in the chair rocking withdrew a wet towel from a basin on the floor next to her chair. She gently wiped Adda's face and forehead and stroked her thin hair, still humming her melancholy tune.

"It takes great strength for her to speak, and she has spoken to you the longest. Do you have from her what you came for?"

"Yes, I have all I need," I said softly.

"I believe that you are the one she has been waiting to see."

"How do you know?"

"Because she breathes no more."

Adda's hand lay limp in mine. I brushed her withered hand against my cheek and kissed it.

"Rest well, Adda." I stood and turned to Franklin's open arms. He enveloped me. Finally I released all the pain I had carried my entire life, each tear bearing with it the weight of my past. With my head on Franklin's shoulder and his arms firmly holding me, we walked out of the bedroom to the front of the house. In the background we could hear the subtle weeping of the two women who remained in the room.

"Are you Frances?" said the gentleman who met us at the front door.

"Yes."

"Then it is a pleasure to meet you."

"What is your name, sir?" I said through my tears.

"I am Eddington. I am the child your grandmother Savannah delivered eighty-five years ago." Eddington extended his hand.

"I am honored to meet you, Eddington," I said, shaking his hand.

"The honor is mine, Ms. Frances. It is good to finally meet the granddaughter of the person my mother speaks about so often."

"You and I have something very special in common."

"Yes, we do. My mother told me the story about how your grandmother sacrificed so much to save the life of my mother as well as my life."

"And I am so grateful to Adda for what she did."

"My mother has told me on many occasions that she had no choice but to save your life."

"What do you mean?"

"You do not fully appreciate the sacrifice that was made to save your life, do you, Ms. Frances? Your grandmother placed the life of a slave above that of a white woman. My mother sacrificed her life to bring a white baby to a place of safety. Maybe one day you will understand when you bear children of your own."

"I hope so, Eddington. I hope so."

Franklin and I sat in the car. No words were spoken as we watched the sun set over the poverty-stricken neighborhood of Macon. The cool of the evening brought more of the elderly out to rest on their front porches, while the children disappeared and the smell of home-cooked meals permeated the atmosphere.

"What are you thinking?" Franklin asked.

"At the moment I don't know what to think or say. I do feel as though I have lived a lifetime in the few moments I spent with Adda."

"You don't have to do or say anything now. We have a long drive back. Just sit back and rest."

Franklin put his arm around me. I leaned comfortably on his shoulder and slept the entire drive back to the hotel.

* * *

It has been a long journey these past few weeks, but it has finally come to an end. I thought it only fitting to remain in Macon for the funeral service for Adda Smith. Five generations of family members were there to tell so many wonderful stories about her life. I was able to glean bits and pieces of what Eddington remembered about my grandmother Savannah and my grandfather John. The one thing Eddington remembered most vividly as a small boy growing up on my grandparents' farm was that before the hired workers began to harvest the land, a prayer would be said, and at the conclusion my grandmother would say, "The earth is the Lord's and its fullness." All other memories of his childhood on the farm or of my mother were too vague for him to recall. The family celebrated through the day and night the transition of their loved one. And I was equally celebrated as if I were a lost relative that had made a long journey home. I now realize the truth behind what Franklin said to me on the train. I should have made this journey years ago.

Today I will leave Atlanta and return to Baltimore, and I will attempt to start leading a normal life for the first time. I've been thinking about what Adda said, that I went not in search of my mother but of myself, of who I am and where I came from. Those questions have now been answered. What now lingers in the shadows of this journey is my future. I have informed Mrs. Wentworth that I will return to the orphanage to say good-bye to the students and pack up the remainder of my belongings. She has been kind enough to recommend me for a teaching position at a private school for gifted children just outside of Boston. I feel like I have been given a new opportunity to start building my own happiness. In just a couple of weeks I have gained more than in my whole lifetime at Weatherford.

Eddington insisted that I return for Thanksgiving to dine with what I call "my extended family." And I can say I have a dear friend, Franklin Bradshaw, without whom none of this would be possible. I will miss him dearly after I leave. I've become quite fond of him. Interesting, now that I know Macon is the place of my roots, it seems odd leaving. For the first time in my life, I feel like I belong.

"I belong," I said out loud as I closed my journal. Sitting on the edge of the bed, I closed my eyes to absorb the morning sun shining through the window of the hotel bedroom. I had pretty much packed everything, and I knew that shortly Franklin would arrive to escort me to the train station in time for him to return to the university campus. I walked over to the sewing basket and took out the glass bottle that started me on my quest. No longer was it simply a glass bottle; it represented a piece of the puzzle that I had been searching for for years.

I held the bottle up to the sunlit window, and the dark brown glass shone like gold against the sun's rays. When I removed it from the sunlight, it returned to its dark and unattractive state. It had become like a solitary beacon in darkness as I held it against my chest. I took the bottle and once again held it up to the light. And there it was. For a brief moment I could not decipher which emotion to act on first--to cry at this revelation or to laugh at another one of my priceless discoveries. I had hidden for years behind Weatherford, believing that it was my refuge when in fact it was my dark prison. I allowed its captivity to wrap me in fear, blinding me from the truth. I believed that my difference was poisonous to anyone who dared to touch me. In silence I fed my intellect, and becoming a teacher at the orphanage was something I had done only to mask the emptiness. An energy surged from inside of me, and years of silence finally escaped from the darkness. I could no longer hold it inside.

"I'm free!" I screamed from the pit of my stomach.

"Frances! Frances! Are you all right?" Franklin yelled through the door.

"Franklin!" I said, opening the door.

"Frances, what is it! What's wrong?"

I wrapped my arms tightly around Franklin's neck. After several minutes I slowly loosened them to look into his wide eyes.

"Franklin, there is something I need to tell you, and I don't know where to begin."

"Just take a deep breath, Frances. It's going to be okay, whatever it is."

"I've been hiding, Franklin. There's a secret I have been afraid to tell anyone for fear that I w-would not be looked upon as normal. My entire life I have been hiding from who I really am."

"There is nothing for you to be afraid of. You have uncovered priceless treasures from your past by coming to Macon."

"But there is something else." I picked up the bottle Adda sent to me and walked over to the window, holding it up so the sunlight could shine through it.

"When I first read the journals as a child, I vowed I would never venture out and leave Weatherford to find the woman who abandoned me on the doorsteps, just so I would have the pleasure of punishing her the day she decided to come back for me. But the day never came. Years passed, and over time my resentment turned to hatred. I loathed having any connection to my past until this small bottle arrived at Weatherford and changed my life. But since leaving on this journey, I found something more important." I paused, choking on my words. "I will never know who Emily was and what became of her, but no matter what became of her, who she was is still a part of me. Now that I know more about my family's history I have to start accepting who I am. I need to find out what I'm supposed to do with, with…"

"Being a prodigy," Franklin interrupted.

"How did you know?" I said, surprised.

"At one point on the train, when you presumed I was asleep, I saw the book that you were reading. You had not mentioned anything about studying to become a doctor. And most women don't casually read advanced books on physics for leisure. And there was one other clue." Franklin took my hands in his. "You've kept your head in a book for so long that you are uncommonly naïve about the things that are happening in the world around you."

"Was it that obvious?"

"Yes, it was." Franklin smiled.

"My life is not going to be the same when I return to Baltimore, is it?"

"Not at first. It will take some time. But I don't think you're going anywhere right now. According to my watch, you have just missed your train."

* * *

Annah stretched her arms over her head and yawned, hoping to read more, but the remaining journal pages were empty. *Another abrupt and inconclusive end to the lives of Franklin and Frances*, she thought. She closed the journal and laid it on top of the other two. Three journals, three lives. Annah felt a lingering connection to her relatives, especially Frances, realizing that she was now the same age that Frances was when she left Weatherford Orphanage. And now, ironically, Annah was returning to Ashton. She held the journals in her hand and inhaled their fragrance. She gazed outside the bay window, focusing on the swing, overshadowed by the full moon. She recalled the last time she spoke to Bethany, and instantly Annah knew what

Bethany was trying to tell her. It had nothing to do with sewing. It was about what was hidden in the basket.

"Well, it's too late, Bethany. The past between you and me is too painful, and I refuse to go back. The only resolve I can give you is to bury it," Annah said as she placed the journals and sewing items back in the basket. She sighed with relief that both the funeral and abortion would be in the past within a couple of days and she would be back in New York, back to her life.

Chapter Eleven

The clouds stretched for miles over the city of Ashton, and the heavy rain had little effect on the few friends, family, and well-wishers who gathered at the repast. Billy Joe's children played on the pine banister and took advantage of the sea of black clothing cramped into the tiny living room by indulging in a game of hide and seek, oblivious to the implication that a family member would no longer be present at future birthdays and holidays. Annah watched from the corner of the room as distant faces greeted her with lukewarm smiles before turning to indulge in idle conversation with someone more familiar. She slowly sipped the hot herbal tea she made in hopes it would settle the nausea in her stomach so that she could eat something without throwing up.

The funeral was uneventful, and she was glad that it was an abbreviated service. It was a closed casket ceremony, which Annah insisted her brother and father agree upon. She thought it best, for no one's sake but her own, to not have burned into her memory the image of Bethany lying in a casket. She felt that her estranged relationship with her mother left enough emotional scars to last a lifetime. Annah slowly sipped her tea until her eyes met those of

Mrs. Gaitlin, who sat behind her during the funeral. Annah recalled the conversation as she knew it had been intended for her ears.

"Bethany's daughter ought to be ashamed of herself. She never once came to visit her mother during her stay in the nursing home," said Mrs. Gaitlin.

"Rumor has it that this is the first time she has been back since she left twenty-five years ago," said someone else.

"I can't imagine what kind of mother she'll make," said Mrs. Gaitlin.

"Hopefully none at all," said another.

Annah dismissed their words and turned her attention to a picture sitting on the fireplace. She picked it up, recalling how it had been taken the day after she graduated from high school. She was standing on the front porch of her home with a suitcase in one hand and her admission papers to Yale in the other. She was dressed in jeans, tennis shoes, and a sweatshirt, with her shoulder-length curly hair stuffed under a ball cap.

"Can you believe that was taken over twenty-five years ago? And you are just as beautiful today. You haven't changed a bit," Edward said.

"You are only saying that because I'm your daughter."

"No, it's true, Annah. You haven't changed. Except you look slightly pale. How are you feeling?"

"I'm fine."

"Are you sure?"

"Edward, now is not the time."

"Then I want you to come with me."

"Where are we going?"

"Now's not the time for questions—just follow me."

Annah followed him as they forded the maze of people. The repast had begun, with a table spread with home-cooked food donated by neighbors. A temporary sedative to dilute their pain, Annah thought. She felt nothing. Outside the heavy rain dwindled temporarily to a light drizzle. The sky was a blend of blue, gray, and orange as the late afternoon gave in to evening.

Annah and Edward sat on the swing and listened to the subtle movement of the wind chimes.

"You haven't said anything all day," Edward said, looking into the distance. "Something is weighing on your mind?"

"I didn't sleep well," Annah said, closing her eyes, hoping to continue sitting in silence.

"You were up late again."

"How did you know?"

"I saw the lamp on in your bedroom."

Annah said nothing.

"You come from a line of amazing women, Annah."

"Edward, let's not pretend. I know why Bethany left me the journals. She hoped it would bring me closer to her."

"One day, when you have children, you will understand…"

"I'm not going to have children," Annah said, sitting on the edge of the swing. "I have a great job. I've just been promoted. I have a wonderful future ahead of me, and my life was fine until… Times are different now. Women have choices. And I choose what I want for my life."

"And what do you choose, Annah?" Edward pressed.

"I choose not to continue this conversation."

"Is this what you do whenever an issue presents itself? You refuse to talk about it?"

"Edward, please…"

Annah felt the nausea rising in the pit of her stomach. Her head felt weightless as a feather floating to the ground. Saliva filled her mouth as she rushed over to the side of the porch just in time to vomit onto the ground. The tea she drank, now mixed with the acid from her stomach, left a rancid taste in her mouth. She stood upright and pressed her face against the cold metal downspout attached to the wooden porch column. It served as a temporary distraction until she vomited again. She held onto the downspout with one hand to keep her balance and with the other hand she wiped the lingering saliva from her mouth. Edward placed his hand gently on her back.

"So, how pregnant are you?"

"How… how did you know?"

"Pale, no appetite, saltine crackers, multiple trips to the bathroom? It wasn't hard to put two and two together."

Annah sat on the edge of the wet porch. The light, warm rain dripped from the roof's edge, saturating her hair and clothes. Her black suede pumps sank into the muddy water below.

"After tomorrow it won't matter."

Edward sat down next to her.

"Does the father know what you intend to do?"

Annah paused before she answered. Her mind drifted back to the rape. For a split second she could see her violator's angry face pressing close to hers and could hear in her mind his vulgar language.

"I don't want this illegitimate child," she said coldly. "I have my whole life ahead of me and I plan on resuming it... so this never happened."

"But what if you are making a big mistake?"

"There are no mistakes in life--there are only choices!" Annah raised her voice. "I chose to leave Ashton! I chose to become a medical doctor! And now *I* choose to get rid of this child."

Edward moved closer.

"Whether you like us or not, or even if you hate the very place where you came from, we are still your family, and that is a truth you will never be able to run from. It doesn't matter how far away you go—the choices you make still affect us here in Ashton. I pray to God that you don't spend the rest of your life regretting it."

"Edward, enough! My decision is final!"

Edward looked up at the rain now pouring from the clouds.

"Give me your hand. We'd better get in before we catch cold."

"No, Edward," Annah said, staring into his eyes. "This choice won't affect anyone. Because this never happened."

"You are as stubborn as you were when you were a child. Listen, Annah, this decision is not like some equation you can simply erase from a chalkboard and do over again. This is different."

Edward slowly turned to go inside without waiting to see if Annah followed. A trickle of rain from her forehead made its way into Annah's mouth. The taste reminded her of the last time she cried.

The evening turned into night, and the spread of food disappeared along with family and friends. Annah watched from the top of the stairs as Edward and Billy Joe stood at the front door saying goodbye to the departing guests, who hastened to their cars in the pouring rain. After changing out of her wet clothes she had remained in her room. She had no interest in joining the line of parading masks.

"There you are, Savannah. Where have you been hiding?" The sarcastic remark from her Aunt Faye didn't make her the least bit uncomfortable. She could hear in Faye's voice the same contempt she had for her as a child.

Annah made her way down the stairs as the last guests offered their condolences. A hug, a pat on the back, and a lowering of the head signaled the end of the procession.

"I need you to help me clean up," Faye said in an almost masculine tone of voice. Annah looked around the kitchen. Clean dishes were stacked neatly on the countertop. The rented tables and chairs were stacked by the back door waiting to be loaded into the truck. The floor initially swept by Faye only lacked a wet mop. Annah looked at her aged aunt. Her red hair, now a glowing orange, betrayed a feeble attempt to cover the gray and maintain her fading stature as a natural redhead. Faye extended the broom to Annah as if accepting it would wipe away years of verbal abuse.

"I think you have it under control. You don't need my help," Annah said, turning away.

"So you're going to walk away just like you walked away from your mother when she needed you?"

Annah turned around. "I don't need to hear this, especially from you."

"Somebody has to tell you. You found time in your life for everybody but the one person who needed you the most."

"You and nobody else in this backwards town is going to make me feel bad about the decisions I made in my life, so I suggest you be quiet and leave it alone."

"All Bethany asked was that you come and visit her, or even call once in a while," Faye continued.

"You really should leave this matter be. You don't know what you're talking about…"

"And you think you've done something great by showing up at her funeral…"

"Stop it!" Annah yelled.

"Well, it's too late! Bethany's dead and she can't hear you ask for forgiveness from the grave!" Faye provoked.

"I'm not going to take any more of this!"

"You are a waste of life!"

Those words caused Annah's mind to travel back to when she was a child. They were the same words Faye said to her at seven when she refused to play with the doll she bought her for Christmas. The memory filled Annah with rage, and Faye's continued belligerence only fueled it. Within seconds, Annah stood coddling the palm of her hand because of the stinging contact it had made with Faye's face. The sound sent Edward and Billy Joe racing into the kitchen to find Annah standing over Faye, who rubbed her red cheek.

"I am no longer the seven-year-old child you can intimidate with your overbearing, controlling personality and insatiable need for attention! The relationship between Bethany and me is none of your business!" Annah stepped back as Faye attempted to regain her composure, her lips tightly pursed.

"I detested you as a child. Now I only pity you."

Annah walked past Edward and Billy Joe and ran up the stairs. The anger continued to boil inside of her like a volcano building up to an eruption. She picked up the pillows on her bed and flung them across the room. She grabbed several books from her closet and threw them at the tapestry Bethany made that hung over her bed. Back and forth she paced across the creaking hardwood floors, rubbing her hands together as if doing so would temper her emotions.

"Annah, it's me," said Edward through the door. Annah stared at the door as he slowly opened it. As soon as he entered the room, she picked up her suitcase and began hastily packing her clothing and shoes.

"Where are you going?" he asked.

"I'm leaving."

"You said your plane doesn't leave until tomorrow."

"I don't care! I refuse to stay here another night."

"It's pouring rain and you know very well the roads leading to the city are flooded."

"I'd rather drown in the rain than spend another night amongst this hideous dysfunction."

"Annah, listen to me!"

"Don't try to talk me out of it, Edward!"

"*Savannah Grace.*" His mild tone caught her attention. He reached over and closed her half-packed suitcase.

"I can't do this anymore," Annah said.

"Do what?"

"This. I can't. I left this place twenty-five years ago, and I refuse to allow people to drag up the past and regurgitate it in my face as if it were yesterday. I don't live in the past, and the longer I stay here, the more I am forced to."

"No one is forcing you. You have to remember your Aunt Faye spent a lot of time taking care of your mother, and seeing you here only reminds her of how much she misses Bethany."

"Well, I'm not going to be her emotional punching bag."

Annah stopped packing and sat on the edge of the bed.

"You see that tapestry? I was six years old when Bethany made it and put it on my wall. I wanted a telescope for my birthday, but she made me a tapestry. You know why? Because no one in this family understands me!"

Edward walked over to the tapestry and studied it as if it were a map.

"You know there is a history behind this," Edward said, running his fingers gently over the stitching. "Your mother started it seven months before your sixth birthday. She would stay up all hours of the night and get up early in the morning before you went to school just so she could finish it in time. One night she came to bed late because she'd had to take out several rows of stitching. When I asked her why she had to take them out, she said, 'Up close you only see the intricate details of the stitching. When you stand back and look at it, the beauty of the picture as a whole draws you closer. I want Savannah to know the beauty of the tapestry up close and far away.'"

"I know what you are going to say: It was her way of showing how much she loved me."

"You decide. But if you ask me, there's not a lot of love in a store-bought telescope."

"I wasn't looking for love. I had this adult brain inside the body of a child, and at times it was just so confusing. I needed someone to help me figure it all out."

"Then you can imagine how she felt. She tried to relate to you as mother to daughter, and you kept responding to her as an adult. She was equally confused. But she did the best that she could with what she had, so you can't blame her for trying."

"Edward, she tried to change me into something that I'm not."

"You probably don't remember, but you and your mother were close at first. Every year in the spring up until you were about five years old, she would sew matching mother-and-daughter outfits and take you to market. Everyone would marvel at how articulate and well-mannered you were. She would buy you an ice-cream cone, and you would tell her that you did not want it on a cone but in a cup just so you wouldn't spoil your dress before taking your picture with her."

"I faintly remember that. I also remember the day things changed between us. Bethany and I had on matching outfits and we were heading away from town. She was very angry with me. I did not understand why she was so angry. She was taking me to Sue Lynn's eighth birthday party. Instead of telling me to have a good time or remember to be kind or mind my manners, she said, 'Can't you for once be a normal little girl?'"

"Annah, she was angry because she knew that she was losing you. You wanted to spend more time with books than

137

you did with her. Your mother knew she hurt you. But by that time, she was dealing with her own illness."

"Then I have one question for you. If you knew she wasn't well, why did you marry her?"

"It was no secret when I met your mother that she was bipolar, but the doctors had given her some medicine and over time she seemed to grow out of it. After your brother was born I noticed that no matter how much they increased her dosage, her illness seemed to be stronger, and slowly it stopped working completely."

"You didn't have to stay. You could have put her in a private psychiatric facility."

"I'm not very proud of it, but I did, soon after you left for college, and three weeks later I went back and took her out. Annah, I just lost one love of my life, and now it feels like I'm going to lose you, and..." Annah opened the suitcase and slowly started packing her things again.

"Edward, this is why I have to leave. You and everyone else keep bringing up the past, and as far as I'm concerned, it's an eyesore I have no desire to revisit."

As Annah looked around to make sure she had packed all her belongings she noticed next to the bed on the floor the sewing basket. She could feel Edward's eyes watching to see if she was going to take it with her.

"I don't regret reading about the women in these journals, and I do feel that I have something in common with them. But I don't need a constant reminder that these women had something that I have no desire for—children. In light of that fact, I will have an abortion before I return to New York. I think it's best that I leave the sewing basket here."

Edward took the sewing basket from Annah and left the room without saying a word. Annah gathered the rest of her belongings and took one last look out the bay window. The swing continued to sway back and forth just as it did when she arrived. As she reached the bottom of the stairs, she felt Edward's hand on her shoulder.

"Annah, I have something for you, but before I give it to you I want you to promise me something."

"Edward, just let me go without bargaining."

"Please, Annah, take this with you. It's a journal your mother kept separate from the others."

"Why are you giving me this now?"

"I just need you to read it. Annah, I've never asked anything of you. Please, promise me that you will read it, completely, before you have the abortion."

"Okay, I promise," Annah said, taking the journal.

"I'm sorry things ended this way. I hope I don't have to wait another twenty-five years before I see you again."

Annah could not respond, for she knew that doing so would give Edward false hope for an apology that she could never allow to leave her lips—not then and not now.

"Say goodbye to Billy Joe and Caroline for me," Annah said as she placed her luggage in the car. Through the mist of raindrops falling on the windshield as she backed out of the driveway, Annah could see the despair on Edward's face. In the car's rearview mirror she watched Edward as he sat down on the porch swing and lowered his head. Soon all that remained was a shadow in the distance.

Annah placed her hand on her chest. She felt an unusual sensation deep inside her, only this time more intense. Her emotions were fully engaged, and no matter how hard she fought, the feeling intensified. *It is only the hormones from the pregnancy. Don't give in, don't give in.* Annah took several deep breaths to keep her eyes from watering, but the feeling would not dissipate. She knew that Edward was hurt by her leaving and she could sense his loneliness.

Ahead in the distance she could see lightning stretching its long fingers across the sky, exposing another approaching thunderstorm. She knew all too well the weather patterns in Ashton, and all flights out of the main airport would be canceled. After an hour's drive in the downpour, Annah felt it would be safer for her to stay in a motel for the night. She pulled the car into the parking lot of a rundown motel off the main highway. Inside, an older gentleman sat at the front desk pouring a cup of coffee, preparing for the long night ahead.

"Excuse me, sir, but do you have any vacancies for the night?"

The gentleman behind the desk stood and without answering her question took out a pen and a ledger.

"Sign here," he said as he squinted through the cigar smoke. "It's thirty-nine dollars a night, forty-two with tax. Cash or credit?"

"I'll pay with cash. And do you have wireless connections in the room?"

"Ma'am, do you know where you are?" he mocked.

Annah looked around the haze-filled lobby. She had forgotten that she was still in the countryside of Ashton and to expect anything other than a TV receiving local stations would be nothing short of a miracle.

"Here's your key. Checkout is at noon," said the gentleman as he placed the money in a drawer and sat down and puffed on his cigar.

Annah returned to her car and drove around to the side of the motel. She lay her head back on the headrest, recounting the event with her Aunt Faye. "She deserved it," Annah said aloud. She had never struck anyone in her life, and remaining composed under extenuating circumstances was something she did not have to work hard at. She felt a soothing sense of satisfaction confronting her aunt. She allowed herself to relish the few moments of Aunt Faye's embarrassment, but none of it could overshadow the intense emotion she felt seeing Edward in the distance sitting on the porch swing in the rain.

Annah managed to find her room. As she fumbled to get the key in the door, she sensed a presence behind her. Her hand grasped the metal doorknob, but her fears stifled her ability to turn it. Her breathing was short and shallow, and her heart pounded in her chest so hard that she could hear its echo in her ears. The rain became drops of anguish dripping from her face.

"Don't turn around, just open the door and go inside," the voice behind her said. Through the coolness of the rain she could feel the heat of his breath on her neck. It was all too familiar to her. Only one thought ran through her mind. *I'll die before I experience another rape.*

"Jesse! Jesse!" came a distant voice. Before Annah could turn and see her would-be oppressor, the odor of his foul breath dissipated and all she saw was a figure running across the road to an open bar.

"I'm sorry," said the gentleman from the lobby. "Jesse is harmless. He wouldn't do anything to you. He's like the village idiot around here, and most guests don't pay him no mind. You forgot your wallet. I was bringing it to you."

Annah turned toward him, her body in shock. She could only stare past him into the night.

"Hey, lady, are you going to be okay?"

Annah swallowed hard, the words barely making it past her lips. "I was raped two months ago, and I will never, ever be okay." She took her wallet from the gentleman and walked back to her car. Leaving the key to her motel room in the door, she drove off.

"I can't take this anymore!" Annah screamed at the top of her lungs as a flood of emotions raged through her like an out-of-control roller coaster.

"I am not going to have this child! I am never coming back to Ashton! I am never coming back, do you hear me, Bethany! I am never coming back!" The speedometer climbed to 60 as the car hydroplaned across the two-lane highway before Annah realized her life was in danger. The windshield wipers struggled to keep up with the downpour of rain. Annah quickly removed her foot from the gas pedal and allowed the car to slow on its own. She turned the wheel to guide the vehicle back on the right side of the road as it rolled to a stop. With everything she had she wailed out a cry to be heard for miles. The overwhelming feelings of anger, hurt, and shame simmering within found their way out. Annah let herself lose complete control, screaming from the pit of her stomach and slamming the steering wheel until her voice gave way to dry, shallow breaths. She swallowed to ease the pain in her throat from her outburst. *This ends now,* she said to herself as she input a destination into the GPS. It was the opposite direction of the airport, but she didn't care. The thought of staying in the same city as the motel pushed her emotions to the limit.

Forty-five minutes later, Annah stepped out of the car into an empty parking lot. The rain had subsided and she allowed herself a fleeting moment of relief. She walked up the steps of the one-story brick building and stared at the sign: "Alternative Pregnancy Clinic." She could see through the glass doors into the dark lobby. The only light within came from the red exit signs above the doorways. The mist gathered on the glass doors ran down over the stenciled hours. "Open—7:00 a.m.," Annah said in a whisper of relief. She walked backed to her car and lay across the backseat in hopes of sleeping until the clinic opened. Her thoughts of Jesse would not allow her to rest. Escaping it was futile. But she felt assured that after the abortion, the incident with Jesse would be put in a casket and buried along with every other painful emotion. *Just a few more hours and this will all end.* Across the highway from the clinic, the dim lights of a coffee shop caught Annah's attention. On the front seat of the car, the familiar fragrance of the journal Edward gave to her echoed her promise to him. After tossing and twisting in the backseat of the car, Annah knew she would not be able to rest. She picked up the journal and walked across the highway into the empty coffee shop. Inside, the décor was an odd blend of a fifties diner and nineties rappers. Black-and-white pictures of Elvis and Frank Sinatra hung side by side, along with photos of Madonna and Michael Jackson. Behind the coffee counter a man and woman who appeared to be in their early twenties chatted about their favorite rap artist. Embroiled in flirtatious banter, they were oblivious to Annah's entrance, and her presence did nothing to break their conversational stride. Annah found a comfortable booth in the far corner of the coffee shop. She glanced once more at her empty surroundings and vowed again she would never return to Ashton. She opened the journal. Unlike the other journals, this one gave no indication in the opening pages who it was written by.

Chapter Twelve

As I look back over my life, I have only one regret. I wish I could turn back the hands of time and live it all over again. Not that my life was not without its difficulties, but as a direct result of choices I made, I have lived a life of loss, misery, loneliness, disappointment, and pain. So why would anyone ever want to relive a life of such anguish? I would have to start at what I know to be my beginning, and hopefully if God grants me the time, I will be able to finish writing in this journal the accounts of my life.

My beginning starts at the end of their story. As a matter of fact, I have heard their story so many times I can almost recite it verbatim. He was my first love, my father, Franklin Bradshaw. Before he met and married my mother, he worked as a professor of pharmacology at a small private university in Atlanta. Frances, my mother, came all the way from Weatherford Orphanage in Baltimore, Maryland, on a quest to find her mother, but what she found instead was the man she would spend the rest of her life loving. Little did my mother know that by her missing the train back to Baltimore, her life would be changed forever.

My parents had a brief courtship. Three months from the day they met each other, they married and settled down to what *they hoped would be a quiet life. But as life is unpredictable, so was their journey together. Nine months from the day they married, I was born. They named me after my father's mother, Leila Marie Bradshaw. It appears that my arrival was no surprise, given the apparent history of women in my family, who always give birth to females and always while in their forties. What is equally interesting, we all have extremely high IQs and are prodigies in medicine.*

My childhood was typical, with the exception that I had an extended family. These family members were students and professors at the university where my father taught. My parents lived close to the campus, and it was not unusual for my mother and I to meet up with my father on a daily basis to have lunch. I particularly loved the attention. And I think the students found it equally amusing to find a six-year-old who could read and comprehend at a college level.

Day in and day out, our lives were pretty much mundane until the day I turned ten and my father received a letter from the head of the university research committee. The university had received a grant from a large pharmaceutical corporation, and with this endowment the university asked my father and mother to head up a team of scientists and researchers to explore the tropical rain forest in South America. My parents' assignment was to bring back samples of exotic plants in hopes of finding a variety of antigens to help treat upper respiratory diseases. My parents were thrilled at the possibility to participate in such an expedition. So, every summer for the next several years, we would take the long journey for a two-month stay in the rain forest. The only time I was unable to go on the excursion with my parents was the summer I turned sixteen and I needed to remain home to prepare for college in the fall.

I begged my parents to let me go with them, but they insisted that I stay behind. It is a day I will never forget. It was a warm summer morning, not a cloud in the sky, and the weather was perfect for traveling. When I close my eyes I can clearly see the black locomotive engine pulling into the train station, and I can feel the steam blanketing the ground, causing the yellow cotton dress that I wore to stick to my perspiring skin. I hugged my parents goodbye with mixed emotions. Anger because they forbid me to go with them, and sadness because I would miss them dearly. We did everything together, and this was the first time our family would be apart for this length of time. My father embraced me and told me that it was going to be their last trip to South America. He and my mother were both getting up in age and were looking forward to retiring and spending their summers in the many places they had planned to visit prior to agreeing to conduct the research. I held on to my father and begged him one last time to please let me come with them, but he insisted my studies over the summer were more important. Unfortunately, it was the last time I saw them. On the day of my parents' expected return, I remained at the station until the last person had disembarked. For two hours I sat staring at the train, believing with all my heart they would eventually appear, until a familiar voice called my name. I turned and found myself looking into the eyes of the chancellor of the university. The tears in his eyes relayed the message he came to deliver. Two weeks later I received a special delivery telegram. It read: "We found the camp of Professor and Mrs. Bradshaw and the team of researchers. The camp raided—bodies nowhere to be found." The news of my parents' fate finally allowed me to exhale and grieve. For many nights that followed I would lie in bed and recall as many wonderful memories as I could of my parents, embellishing them all with happy endings. On one of the nights that I could not sleep, I took the journals from my mother's sewing basket and read them over and over until dawn. I found solace in my family's past. From that time forward it became my own private ritual to recite several passages from memory. Even though my parents were gone, reading the journals helped me feel connected to them. The one phrase I would read over and over was from my great-great-grandmother, who said her mother told her that she was different so she could make a difference. In commemoration of my parents' lives, I have vowed that I will do whatever I can to be sure I preserve my family's heritage.

The memorial service for my parents was attended by hundreds of students, government officials, and all members of the faculty and governing board of the university. I even received a personal letter from the mayor of Atlanta offering his condolences. It was a great day of commemoration. Three days after the service, I packed my bags and left Atlanta, deciding that it was the best thing for me emotionally, and I enrolled in a small private university in Connecticut. Soon my days and evenings were filled again with study, and within five years, I completed my undergraduate studies and medical school and was working at a local veterans hospital to complete my internship and residency.

On my first day as an intern I was given the assignment of changing the dressing on a patient. His name was Carrington Ransom, and his chart indicated he had fought in World War II. The hospitals during that time were filled with men recovering from the long war. Many were amputees with recurring infections and had been placed in the hospital to prevent the infection from spreading further. Carrington was no different. I stood at the foot of his bed for a few moments and watched him sleeping. His face had a few scars, possibly souvenirs from the war. He was only 26 years old, but he looked every bit of a man in his mid-thirties. I lifted up the blankets to check his wound.

"If you're looking for my leg, let me know when you find it. It's been missing for quite some time now," Carrington said with a straight face as I stood with my head peering under the bedcovers, dumfounded.

There was an awkward yet comfortable silence between us. "It's okay, you can laugh. It's a joke," he said. We both broke into laughter, which contagiously sprouted into love, and after I completed my internship and residency, I became Mrs. Carrington Ransom III.

Soon after we married, Carrington and I moved to Birmingham, Alabama, where I opened up a private practice as an obstetrician. Carrington worked with a team of physicians and specialists to develop state-of-the-art prosthetics for amputees. We loved our life, and our profession fueled our passion. Now although we had no immediate plans for children, a year after we were married I became pregnant. Despite the popular demand, and the rarity of a woman working for herself in the 1950s, I continued my private practice for as long as I was able to conduct business. As far as my pregnancy, I loved every moment—the morning sickness and the unusual cravings of smothering everything I ate in steak sauce. Even going to the bathroom five times in the middle of the night I found amusing. And Carrington--he was the perfect, attentive husband, and I had no doubt that he would be an even better father.

Six weeks before the birth of our child, our home was ready, the baby's room was decorated, and we were excited and felt prepared to be parents. We were particularly thrilled because I come from a generation of women who gave birth in their mid to late forties. I broke the mold and gave birth to a beautiful baby girl on July 23, 1953. We named her Bethany Gabrielle Ransom. Bethany was the heartbeat of our home. At 16 months she was reading, and by the time she was five she could read at a 12th grade level. As delightful of a child as Bethany was, we noticed she started showing unexplained signs of aggression and anger as she approached six. At first we thought perhaps she was exhibiting these signs because of her high IQ, so we did everything possible to keep her occupied by stimulating her intellect. But we found it only exaggerated her aggression. Soon, we were forced to reach the realization that something was wrong with our Bethany that our love as parents could not fix. It wasn't until after Bethany was expelled from three different schools that we knew we could no longer mask the truth. We took her to a child psychologist in Birmingham, and he confirmed that Bethany had an acute manic-depressive disorder. The doctor asked about our family history, and neither Carrington nor I knew of any immediate family members who exhibited this type of behavior. But when I told him that on my side of the family we have four generations of gifted children, he theorized that it was a gene that may have lain dormant for generations before suddenly deciding to make its debut in our dear Bethany.

Be that as it may, Bethany's medical challenges changed our whole lives. Without any regard to my career as a doctor, I resigned my practice and remained devoted to loving, caring and doing everything in my power to make sure Bethany had the best possible life. Although it was very hard, needless to say, Bethany was a breath of fresh air for Carrington and I. We never knew what kind of mood she would wake up in. There were days she was vibrant, energetic, and creative. Then there were days she would regress to her violent behavior. The most trying times came when Bethany would wake up screaming from her night terrors. It could take us hours to settle her down. There was one night when Carrington and I tried everything to get her to come out of it. Even with applying cold towels to her face, she continued screaming, closing her eyes tight for fear that if she opened them she would see her tormentor. The only thing I could do was hold her close in my arms and sit in the rocking chair and pray that God would take it away.

Bethany's night terrors went on for what seemed like years. Carrington and I became increasingly tired and weary of the battle, beaten down by sleep deprivation and frustration. And to add to our plight, we were judged and criticized by our neighbors and Carrington's family members, who attempted to coerce us into putting Bethany away. At times it did seem a convenient solution because we had so many unanswered questions. But Carrington and I decided that Bethany was a gift to us. And we focused on directing Bethany's life towards her good. My days were exhausting and my nights tiresome, but I loved my daughter and she needed me. I wouldn't understand how much I needed her until we received an unexpected report from the doctor. Carrington had taken a bad fall, and his upper thigh developed an infection to the point that he had to be hospitalized. For four weeks Bethany and I went daily to the hospital to spend time with Carrington. He was on a complete antibiotic drip, and after no signs of improvement, the doctors switched to a more potent antibiotic, but the infection continued to spread to his hip. The doctors did not understand how the strain of infection mutated so quickly, and they were running out of options for treatment. It wasn't until 3:00 am on the morning of November 5th that the infection resolved. My dear Carrington passed away. When we arrived at the hospital, Bethany was forbidden to see her father, but she insisted. From the door of ICU I watched as Bethany walked into the room and unabashedly climbed up on the bed. She stared at him for a moment in silence, and then she kissed her father on the cheek. She climbed back down and came over to me and took me by the hand and said, "Don't worry, Mommy. Daddy is just going to sleep for a long time now."

The weeks following the funeral were difficult. Everything in our home reminded me of Carrington, and I felt Bethany and I needed a change of scenery and a fresh start. To this end, I sold Carrington's ownership of the prosthetic business to his business partner, our home, and all of our furnishings. I didn't have in mind moving to any particular place, just somewhere far away and peaceful. Our new beginning started in a small country town just outside of Birmingham. I purchased a large single-story, plantation-style house with a small one-bedroom guesthouse on two and a half acres of land. It was perfect. Within a couple of months we had adjusted to our new lifestyle. We had a few chickens for fresh eggs, a rooster to wake us up in the morning, a vegetable garden, a dog, a cat, and a rabbit that Bethany fondly named Herman, which was the name of Carrington's childhood hamster. Best of all, the neighbors were friendly. I found it amusing that city people would move to the country and that country people likewise wanted to live in the city. Our conversations served as a form of mutual education. Bethany quickly acclimated to her new surroundings as well as her new medications. The quiet atmosphere soothed her, and her erratic behavior diminished and I was able to enroll her in the local elementary school. We had developed a daily routine of me waiting for her each day after school on the front porch with fresh squeezed lemonade and homemade oatmeal raisin cookies. She and I would sit in the rocking chairs and talk about her day. I enjoyed the peace of mind we had finally achieved. That all changed one day when Bethany did not return home from school at the normal time. Just as I ran to the car to go look for her, I saw her small frame and long blond hair coming down the road. But she was not alone. She was holding the hand of a tall dark man. His name was Henry Moore, and he had moved to our town from Mississippi to help his older brother farm the land he had newly acquired. Unfortunately, his brother did not keep to his promise, and Henry was going from house to house offering his services as a handyman. That's how he ran into Bethany. Bethany was outspoken and convincing, and she readily promised Henry a job to fix up our house, going so far as to assure him he could stay in our guesthouse. Despite my initial reservations, Henry turned out to be God sent. Within six months our house was painted, inside and out. Our two acres of land were landscaped, and Henry rebuilt the chicken coop to include a place for rabbits and ducks. Soon Henry's handiwork developed into a small business, and within another few months he was able to pay off the back rent he owed us.

On rainy days when Henry was forced to set aside his work, he and I would sit on the front porch, drink lemonade, and laugh about our cultural differences. The more time we spent together, the closer we became friends, and in time our friendship turned into affection. It was five years from the day Henry moved into the guesthouse that he asked me to marry him. I accepted his proposal, but we both knew our marriage would not be looked upon favorably by our town.

As it turned out, it would prove to be dangerous for Henry. Racial tension in the South was brewing, and we needed to take whatever precautions were necessary to protect ourselves. When we told Bethany she was elated, and during Bethany's spring break, Henry and I flew to a city in Nevada, married, and honeymooned at a beautiful resort in the desert. After we returned, we managed to live our lives secretly as husband and wife and decided it was best to wait until Bethany finished her senior year of high school before we moved to a place that was more accepting of interracial marriages. Bethany had known Henry since she was a child, and his position as her only father figure was evident in their relationship. Henry loved Bethany as if she were his own daughter. Our lives, were perfect—or so we thought. I will never forget the day I lost the second love of my life.

It was just two weeks before Bethany was due to graduate from high school. I was in the kitchen preparing lunch for Henry when I saw Bethany and a young man getting out of a car and heading toward the backyard, where Henry was putting a fresh coat of paint on the fence. His name was Edward George Kentwell, and he was a fine young man. He and Bethany spent a lot of time together during their senior year, but Henry and I noticed after the spring dance the two of them began to develop a deep admiration for each other. I never asked Bethany, but it was apparent she was fond of him. Every morning at breakfast it seemed like every other word that came out of her mouth was "Edward." They were inseparable. One would think they were connected at the hip. I watched Bethany and Edward from the kitchen window, and even at a distance it was plain to see Edward was captivated by her. She had grown into a beautiful woman. Moments later Edward rushed through the kitchen door and proclaimed he had asked Henry for Bethany's hand in marriage. Henry gave his blessing, and now I needed to seal it with my approval. From the kitchen I could see Henry affectionately swinging Bethany around in his arms just as he did when she was a little girl. Bethany giggled and laughed, yelling at the top of her lungs, "Put me down!" Henry continued to swing her faster. It all ended with the sound of a gunshot, followed by Bethany's piercing scream, which lingers in my ears to this day. I rushed to the side of my beloved Henry where he lay on the ground. Across our backyard I could see our neighbor, Mr. Beechum, jumping over the white picket fence separating our property. He yelled out to Bethany, "Are you okay, little lady? That should teach that boy not to touch one of us." With no regard for her own life, Bethany attacked Mr. Beechum, leaving scratches that ran from his forehead to his neck. Her vengeful fight was held back by Edward, but Bethany stood directly under Mr. Beechum's nostrils, glaring, unmovable through clenching teeth. "That is no boy you shot. That man is my father!"

I held Henry in my arms, looking deeply into his eyes. With the last of his failing strength, he gently stroked my face. He couldn't speak, but his eyes conveyed more than words ever could, until he drew his last breath. Two days later I buried my second husband. At the funeral there were no family members other than Bethany, Edward, and myself to mourn our loss. No letters or telegrams from friends sending their condolences, no repast. The church we had come to call our family refused to allow the services to be conducted because Henry was not white. Henry's brother and family members were afraid to hold the service at their church for fear of what would become of them. We said our final words at the gravesite, and from that day the neighborhood and community never treated us the same. We were called every name under the sun. The place I had come to love, to spend the rest of my days, had become a place of contention. Our home became our jail. We were grateful for a brief respite from our time of mourning to attend Bethany's high school graduation. As class valedictorian, Bethany was given the opportunity to attend the school of her choice. I was so proud of her. Bethany had come through many challenges in life, and learned how to take her disability and turn it around to her advantage. One month after her graduation, Bethany and Edward were married, and the three of us prepared to move to California, where Bethany would attend the University of California at Berkley. It was the same day I received the news from the doctor-I was going to have a baby. With this unexpected news, Edward and Bethany insisted it would be better for her to forgo a year of college and make sure I was comfortably settled and to help out with the baby. We all agreed on the plan and were looking forward to moving within a year. But things changed for the worse. I was carrying the child of a black man. Our home was broken into and burglarized, and our windows were broken so many times that eventually Edward stopped repairing them and simply kept them boarded up. I refused to lose sight of our goal. My mother taught me that adversity builds determination, and determination builds character, and character, hope.

Time did seem to slow down while I was pregnant. I had ample time to knit outfits for the baby since I knew a nursery was out of the question in light of the move. Edward was good with his hands, and he built a beautiful cradle. Bethany made sure I ate correctly, and we walked every evening for exercise. We found a midwife who was willing to help deliver the baby *since I was not accepted at a hospital for Blacks and turned away at the local hospital for whites. One month before I gave birth, we had a buyer for our home, and soon our lives were spent busily packing for the move. It was then that I pulled out the sewing basket containing the journals. I had never read them to Bethany, and it was time she knew about our family history. It was one evening after dinner that I sat her down and told her the stories in the journals. Bethany marveled at the fact that we had over four documented generations of women with extraordinarily high IQs. But it was the statement that Bethany made I will never forget. "It's not just a baby a woman carries, but a life source."*

Annah stopped reading. She laid the journal on the table and hesitated before turning the page. "Life source," she said aloud as she placed her hand on her stomach. She could feel her body changing. There was an unusual tingling sensation in her breasts, and her mouth produced an unusual taste. She tried to dismiss the thought that she was carrying a life source. She allowed her mind to flash back to the rape, for in that memory were wrapped the emotions of pain and bitterness. Annah attempted to recall the vomiting in hopes it, too, would drive out any thoughts of delaying the abortion. She quickly dismissed any feelings of attachment to the child she was carrying. She recited over and over in her mind that she was making the right decision. She had been violated, and she did not want to live with the pain any longer than she had to. Abortion was her only recourse.

Annah removed her cell phone from her purse and looked at it. Within a few hours the clinic would open and she would have the entire horrific event behind her.

The stress her body had incurred began to catch up to her. She was sleepy and longed for a place to rest until the clinic opened. Since she sat down only two other customers had come in for some coffee, and now the café was empty. Her mind grew hazy as she fought to stay awake. The rain outside the café softly tapped against the window, and it lulled her to sleep.

Chapter Thirteen

Annah opened her eyes, and over her stood a woman who appeared to be in her late sixties holding a pot of coffee.

"Ma'am? Are you okay? Ma'am? Do you need me to get someone to help you?" Annah was disorientated. She sat up and looked out the window of the café. She could see the alternative pregnancy center across the highway. She rubbed her hand across her forehead and asked the woman in a groggy voice, "What time is it?"

"Half past seven."

"I've got to get going." Annah gathered her purse and got up from the booth to leave. By the time she reached the door, she could hear the older woman calling to her.

"Ma'am, you left this." The woman handed Annah the journal.

"Thank you. In my haste I forgot about it. Oh, I'm sorry, I forgot to leave you a tip."

"No, you do not owe me anything."

"I was really tired, and I appreciate your hospitality."

"Ma'am, I know this is none of my business, but I make it a point to let everyone know just how final this decision is," the woman said, looking out at the clinic. "I have seen them come and go from all ages and walks of life. The sad thing is that the women who go through with it really believe that their life will return to what it was… before."

Doing her best to ignore such advice, Annah stepped outside the café. The clinic across the highway appeared monumental against the dark gray skies. She caught a glimpse of white clouds far off in the east and the morning sunrays weaving through them. She knew the storm was passing. She looked back through the glass doors of the café at the waitress staring at her, attempting to penetrate her soul. She avoided the stare-down and let out a deep sigh of relief as turned and crossed the highway.

Entering the abortion clinic, Annah's heart raced with anticipation. The aroma of cleaning solution mixed with the smells of a dental office filled her nostrils. A wave of nausea arose, but this time she had nothing to vomit.

"Can I help you?" said the receptionist.

"I don't have a scheduled appointment, but I would like to utilize your services for an… an…" Annah struggled with her words.

"Abortion," said the woman.

"Yes, I would like to schedule this procedure," Annah said, trying to conceal her uneasiness.

"You are fortunate. Two people just cancelled because of the bad weather. Here, I need you to complete this form." The woman handed Annah a clipboard. "When you are finished with the form, you will go to the restroom behind this door and leave your urine sample with your name on it in the opening just behind the toilet. I need you to sign these release forms before we take you in. The cost is $650."

"How long? How long will it be before…"

"After we get the results of your test, and provided there are no complications, you will be in and out within thirty minutes, depending upon how far along you are."

"I have a request," Annah said under her breath so as not to be heard by another woman standing nearby. "I would like this to be kept strictly confidential."

"The only information we require is a contact name in the event something happens."

"Thank you, but I prefer that not even the person I leave as a contact be called unless… unless a decision needs to be made concerning my well-being, and he will know what to do in the event of my demise."

"Return the forms to the front desk when you are done." The receptionist's robotic response left Annah in question concerning her directions. She hoped there would be no complications. But as a doctor, Annah knew sometimes the unexpected happens. Her mind drew upon her experience with her patient Christina. *What if there are complications? What if I die? Is it really worth it?* The thought of not ever waking up from the procedure tugged heavily at her heart.

Annah walked to a far corner of the room to find a seat, and her palms began to sweat. *Just breathe,* she told herself over and over. *You can do this. Nothing is going to happen to you. Just relax.* To ease her discomfort she focused on imagining what her life would be like after the abortion. She would return to New York and resume her new position at the hospital. No one would ever come to know that she left town to attend her mother's funeral or have an abortion. Annah tugged at the top she wore, grateful for her slender frame. Her body showed no external signs that she was pregnant, with the exception that her bras had become tighter, and she had taken to wearing layers to conceal her fullness.

More than her performance as a cardiologist, Annah knew how to separate her feelings and emotions from facts. The facts added up to one decision: Get rid of the evidence, and time will dissolve any residue of the pain.

Annah returned from the bathroom and gave the completed forms to the receptionist.

"Cash or credit?" said the receptionist.

"Credit." Annah searched in her wallet for her credit card. She pulled out the items from her purse and laid them on the counter.

"There it is. It's stuck in your notebook," said the receptionist.

Annah opened the journal to the page where the credit card marked the spot where she had stopped reading.

"Ma'am, I need your payment."

"Yes, of course, here's my card."

"We'll call you when we are ready for you."

"Thank you."

Annah returned to her seat in the corner. There were three other women who sat in the waiting room. One of them appeared to be in her early teens. She lowered her head after making eye contact with Annah. The tissues that filled her hands overflowed into her lap. Judging from their resemblance, the woman who sat next to her appeared to be her mother, and she sat silently as the young girl continued to fill tissues with her tears. The other woman looked to be in her late twenties and was dressed as if she spent her entire life in the red-light district of Amsterdam. The distinguished looking man sitting next to her was well into his fifties. The camouflage of dark clothes, ball cap, and designer sunglasses he wore demonstrated that his public and private lifestyles had converged in the lobby of an abortion clinic. The woman's level of comfort with the surroundings and her quaint conversations with the receptionist and clinicians pointed toward the fact this was not her first visit.

Annah turned her mind to the journal she held in her hand. Had she not promised Edward she would finish it before she had the abortion she would be sitting thinking only of the future. She took in a deep breath, exhaled, and opened the journal. Her heartbeat quickened as she read the first few lines, which struck her as not continuous with where her grandmother Leila had previously left off.

I can feel it. Life slowly leaving me. I wish I had more time. There is so much more that needs to be said. With whatever energy I have, I will write as much as I can. I had the baby three days ago. The delivery was very difficult, and the heavy bleeding still continues. Bethany and Edward are here around the clock caring for me. It's been hours since the midwife left to find a doctor to come to the house. I hope that the doctor returns before it's too late. By this week's end, we will move to Ashton, Nebraska, the home of Edward's grandparents. Edward said they live in a small town on a farm, and that it's a great place to raise a family and free of the racial tension that we are experiencing here in Birmingham. Edward's grandparents have lived there for years, and thank God they will receive us with open arms.

I have convinced Edward and Bethany that once I am settled, they will move on to California so that Bethany will be able to enroll in college before the fall admission deadline. Bethany insists on forgoing her scholarship, but I won't have it. She has worked too hard and has come too far. Her life is with Edward now, and I want them to make the most of it. However, truth be told, I've decided that if I don't make it, this journal will stand as a record of my last will and testament. I had two wonderful men whom I loved with all of me. Bethany has grown into a fine young woman, and Edward will take good care of her. Despite her condition, he has vowed to me that he will never leave her. I'm grateful that my daughter has found someone to love her unconditionally.

I will leave on this earth three priceless possessions: the journals, passed down from my relatives, and my children. Within each child lives the legacy that has been passed down through many generations, from woman to woman. I want my children to know that there are no guarantees that life is going to be easy. But if you choose life, you will accomplish what you were put on this earth to do, and that is to make a difference.

I leave this legacy for my two daughters, Bethany Gabrielle Kentwell and Savannah Grace Moore.

Annah's eyes opened wide. She laid her hands on her chest, letting out short, quick breaths as she gasped for air. Her mind had already calculated the date, and her emotions responded to the reality. Annah's whole body quivered. The journal she held in her hand fell to the floor. She became lightheaded, and using the only strength she had left she leaned over and rested her head against the wall, her eyes resisting their natural inclination to blink.

Shocked, Annah reached down and picked the journal up from the floor and turned back to the last page she read.

She wanted to believe that her grandmother intended to say something else. She turned the page slowly, prepared to read more. Page after page was blank. On the last page of the journal two pages were glued together. As she pulled the pages apart, a small black-and-white photo fell out. On the backside of the picture were the words, "To my sister Savannah — this is the only picture I have of your father Henry and our mother together. Love Bethany." Slowly Annah turned it over to see a woman standing on the porch of a ranch-style house. Annah had her same nose and tall, thin frame. Behind her stood a man whose skin was the color of dark soil. His muscular arms wrapped around her mother's waist, and their faces met cheek to cheek. In him Annah could see her full lips, round face, and eyes. Annah brushed her fingertips slowly over the photo as if she could reach back in time and touch their faces.

"Ms. Kentwell, we are ready for you," said the receptionist, impatient that Annah had not responded the first two times she called her name.

"Already?"

"Yes. We had another patient cancel, so it's your turn."

Annah stood slowly.

"Take this information with you through the double doors, and the nurse will give you further instructions."

Annah took the picture of her parents, placed it back inside the journal, and walked through the double doors to another small reception area.

"Ms. Kentwell? Ms. Kentwell?"

"Yes."

"Follow me," said the nurse.

Annah followed slowly behind the nurse, she was unable to focus. Missing pieces and questions about her family ran through her mind. Now she knew why her olive-toned skin and curly hair were different from Edward's and her brother Billy Joe's straight blond hair. She had Bethany's thin frame and shared their mother's features, as the picture clearly showed. The question now was why was it kept a secret for so long. Annah's mind could not comprehend the facts, and she needed some resolution.

Annah removed her clothing and dressed in a gown. She placed her personal belongings in the locked cabinet in the room but held onto the journal. She took out the picture for one last look at her parents. Her mind filled with more questions, and she had no one to answer them. She read again the inscription on the back of the photo.

"Are you ready, Ms. Kentwell," said the nurse.

"Yes… I'm ready." Annah laid the picture and journal on the exam table. She felt her heart beating faster. *You are making the right decision,* she repeated to herself. *You were victimized. You have your whole career ahead of you.*

"Relax, Ms. Kentwell, and before you know it, it will all be over with, as if nothing ever happened," said the nurse.

Annah lay on a gurney and was wheeled to another room for the procedure. It was only a matter of minutes, but it seemed as if everyone was moving in slow motion. The nurse inserted the IV in her arm. To her left she could see the doctor donning the surgical mask as he checked his instruments. *Am I making the right decision? I have so many unanswered questions about my family…*

The doctor stood at Annah's feet. "Please place your feet in the stirrups," he said.

This child will always be a reminder of a horrible incident.

"Ms. Kentwell, I promise you, when you wake up, you won't feel any different," said the nurse.

What if this is a mistake?

"*Remember our family legacy,*" came a voice from the pages of the journal.

They were the last words that Annah heard.

Chapter Fourteen

The recovery room was barren. Monitors blinked in perfect sequence beneath the flickering florescent light above the bed. The smell of antiseptic and rubbing alcohol mixed with the cool air from the air conditioner only added to the sterile environment. Annah's heart rate and blood pressure were normal and her breathing steady. Her eyelids were heavy, and she slowly raised them as she regained consciousness. "Remember our family legacy." The voice in her head caused her to open her eyes wide. It was the same voice she heard just before the abortion. She closed her eyes again and could see in her mind visions of each woman she read about in the journals. She could see time passing before each woman, and with each passing moment, as each woman completed her journal, she placed it in the sewing basket, passing it to the next generation. As the basket was handed to her mother Leila, Annah envisioned both her parents holding the basket in their arms. Through their laughter and joy she could feel the love her parents shared and the love they felt for her. She could hear her mother's soothing voice telling her father how happy they were to have such a beautiful daughter. Then the words rang out from her mother's lips that shifted everything in Annah's mind. "I hope she remembers that the life she will carry someday will make a difference." The voices and faces faded into darkness. Annah opened her eyes.

"Oh, no! Oh, God! What have I done!" Annah looked over at the heart monitor next to the bed and could see her blood pressure rising. Her stomach contracted. She placed her hand underneath the blanket to massage her abdomen, hoping to ease the pain. Her hands encountered something damp. Removing the blankets, Annah witnessed the horror of what had taken place.

"Oh, God! Somebody, help me! Please, somebody help me!" Annah yelled out. "No! No! What have I done! What have I done!" Annah screamed over and over.

"Ms. Kentwell, Ms. Kentwell," the nurse said, pulling Annah's hands from her face.

"I'm sorry!" Annah said, squeezing the nurse's hand. "I made a horrible mistake!

"Try to relax, Ms. Kentwell," the nurse said, patting Annah's hands to calm her down.

"You don't understand. I wasn't supposed to have an abortion. I-I was supposed to have this baby."

"It's okay," said the nurse. "Now calm down and try to relax."

"I knew it was a mistake," Annah continued. "But I didn't pay attention!"

"Why do you say it was a mistake?"

"Because…" Annah paused. She took a deep breath. "Because I have been reading about this baby for the past five generations in my family."

The nurse gave Annah a puzzled look. "The full effects of the anesthesia have not completely worn off, and you are not quite coherent."

"I made a mistake! Do you hear me? I made a mistake and now I can't take it back, it's too late!"

"Ms. Kentwell, please lie back and try to relax," the nurse said softly.

"You don't understand. I was supposed to give life... for the next generation. Now none of us will ever know what our lives could have become."

"Ms. Kentwell, I don't know what you are talking about, the nurse said, removing Annah's hands from her face. "Look at the monitor." Annah turned her head. "What does the heartbeat register at?"

"One forty-five."

"Ms. Kentwell, that's not your heartbeat. That is the heartbeat of your baby."

"Baby? But-but...I saw...on my gown."

Annah removed the blankets and placed her hand on the fetal monitor on her abdomen.

"You were just having a bad reaction to the anesthesia."

"You mean..." Annah hesitated and choked on her words.

"Yes, your baby is alive."

"I thought it was too late. What happened?"

"Apparently, you were not supposed to have an abortion. That's what happened."

"But how? I remember, I heard this voice."

"You didn't hear just any voice. It was your voice. I was standing right there. Before you went under I heard you say, 'I want this baby.' I was not the only one who heard it.

The doctor heard you also. Then he said, 'We'd better wait on this one.'"

Annah placed her hand on her stomach and softly caressed it. "She's alive," she whispered.

"You can tell it's a girl by the heartbeat?"

"No... a relative from 1798 told me." Annah smiled.

"Interesting," said the nurse, even more puzzled. "You will be coherent in about an hour, Ms. Kentwell."

"I'm having a baby," Annah said to herself, as if in disbelief. "I am going to have a baby."

"Ms. Kentwell. There is something else I need to tell you."

"Don't worry, I won't ask for my money back."

"That's not it. Because of your condition..."

"Condition? What condition?"

"It's not critical, but your blood test shows that you are extremely anemic."

"I had a feeling that was the case. I don't usually have headaches, and I wake up fatigued even after a full night's rest."

"We needed to take some precautions, so we called your emergency contact. He is waiting in the lobby."

"Does he know?"

"No. It's confidential information. And besides, I'm sure he would much prefer hearing it directly from you."

Annah's eyes scanned the room as if words were hidden in the fabric of the walls that could express to Edward how she felt. She had been so adamant about having the abortion, but her mind had changed and she didn't know how to convey it to Edward. She did know one thing for certain:

that her relationship with him would not change now that she knew the truth.

"If you are ready, I'll send him in."

"I'm ready." Annah gently massaged her stomach as Edward walked into the room. They stared at each other for what seemed like minutes. Annah's sudden sobbing broke the silence, her tears flowing like the rain pouring down on Ashton. Edward walked over and sat on the side of the bed and enveloped her in his arms, just as he had when she was a little girl.

"Nothing has changed," Edward said, "You will always be my little girl. It's going to be okay." Edward whispered to her, "I will never judge you for this decision. I'm just glad you are safe and alive."

Annah lifted her head from his shoulder and muffled through her tears, "I didn't go through with it."

"You mean… you're still pregnant?"

"Yes, I am."

"You did the right thing."

"It wasn't me that made the decision alone. If I hadn't read the journals I would have made the biggest mistake in my life."

"I'm glad you changed your mind."

"It sealed my decision. I know now that this baby is here for a reason." Annah's eyes lit up and settled on the chair on the far side of the room. Edward followed her gaze, picked up the journal that sat on top of her clothes, and placed it in her hands. Annah turned to the last page of the journal and pulled out the picture of her parents.

"All these years, Edward. Why did you wait until now to tell me the truth?"

"Bethany wanted to tell you sooner, but I chose not to."

"Why?"

"I didn't want her to suffer any more loss than she already had. The man she knew as her father was shot, and she was the one who found your mother dead."

"I want to know how it happened."

"It was in the middle of the night. She noticed the light was still on in your mother's room, so she went in to check on the two of you. You were lying in the cradle sleeping peacefully, and your mother was sitting up in bed with this journal in her lap. What you read was her last entry. Bethany was strong, though, and she was prepared. Your mother told her before you were born that if she didn't make it, Bethany was to raise you as her own daughter, but to promise her that when you were old enough she would tell you the truth. I feared that if I had told you, it would be taking away the one thing she lived for."

"You two had Billy Joe."

"Yes, we did, but there was no greater joy for your mother than knowing she had a daughter, someone she could pass the legacy that had been passed to her from her mother."

"The swing, the sewing basket, the journals. All those days that I came home from school and Bethany would be sitting there, waiting to tell me about my heritage."

"She wanted you to hear it from her so that she could answer any questions you had about your mother and father and the journey of the other women in your family. After you left for college, every year on your birthday she would wake up in the morning and make sure the house was cleaned. She would go in your room and remove the bedding and wash it so that it would be fresh and clean for your return. By lunchtime there would be sweet tea and fresh-baked bread on the table. She would get the sewing basket and sit on the swing for hours, just waiting. Every time she saw a car in the distance coming down the road, her face would light up with expectation, hoping finally that she could personally give you the sewing basket and tell you the truth about your mother. When I would check on her late in the evening she would be sitting there on the porch quietly reading through the journals. She would look up at me with her big brown eyes and say, 'She'll come next year, Edward, I'm sure of that.' She did this for ten years, until the day I allowed her to lapse in taking her medication. From then on, it was on your birthday that she would sit on the porch and embroider from sunup until sundown. In time, all she could recall was that she had a little girl she loved. I'm sorry Savannah. I was wrong to keep the journals from you all these years."

"No, Edward. It's not your fault. All these years I thought I was the missing piece of this puzzle, and all along the puzzle has been waiting for me to find myself."

Annah looked down at her stomach. "What am I supposed to do now?"

"You've already made the first step, you're having a baby."

"Edward, I have over forty years of repressed feelings. Less than three hours ago I found out that my father is my brother-in-law and my mother is really my sister. My biological father is African American and I'm sitting in an abortion clinic, pregnant. I'm smart enough to admit that there are some in between steps in this process. I need to start picking up the pieces of my life and stop hiding and put things in proper order. I'm going to fly back to New York and meet with my boss, Dr. Rivas, and let him know I need to take some additional time off so that I can sort this all out."

"What about your promotion? Do you think your boss will understand?"

"Dr. Rivas is pretty intuitive, and he's not just my boss, he's my mentor... and my friend. And as I get closer to the time of delivery, I may need you to come to New York and stay with me. I'll even put a swing on my balcony where we can relax and you can make sweet tea and fresh homemade bread when I get too fat to get up and make it for myself."

"I think I know of a place just like that, and it's been waiting for you." Edward smiled.

Chapter Fifteen

May 18, 2055

The room is filled with reporters, cameras, renowned leaders in the medical field, and government officials from around the country...

The ceremony had begun, and Annah stopped writing in her journal and turned her attention toward the stage. Annah could see sitting to the right of the stage an African-American woman searching the audience with her eyes. It was then that Annah and Kathleen's eyes met. Kathleen smiled warmly and Annah returned the smile with a nod. Annah's heart beat fast in her chest as the emcee at the podium announced Kathleen's continued breakthroughs in the fields of pediatrics, obstetrics, and gynecology.

"Now I present to you Dr. Kathleen Clarice Whitman-Steinberg," said the emcee.

Kathleen stood and walked to the podium carrying the sewing basket in her hand.

"Ladies and gentlemen, words cannot express how honored I am to receive this prestigious award today. This award represents the commitment and hard work that has been dedicated not just to medical science, but to the lives of women all over the world who now have a choice, choose life. In the United States alone there are over fifty million women who are unable to conceive. Medical research findings show that this rate is increasing by the thousands daily. These women year after year ask themselves, 'Will I ever be able to become pregnant?' What is more alarming is that in the United States there are over five million abortions conducted in the first trimester. The statistics are even more alarming when you factor in the number of abortions conducted around the world. But today medical science can give women who are infertile an option. We are now able to take the first trimester embryo and transplant it directly into an infertile womb. Through administering AWAKE, the embryo is able to thrive and grow in the transplanted womb as in any normal pregnancy, with less than one percent ending in a miscarriage. This medical breakthrough can essentially eradicate first trimester abortions. I want to share with you my story," Kathleen continued. "I have devoted my entire life to the practice and research of medicine. It was my first love and has been with me since I was a small child. But my journey did not begin when I was born forty-five years ago." Kathleen paused and took a deep breath. "This medical breakthrough was imbedded in the DNA of my five times great-grandmother Kathleen Clarice O'Brien, who carried it to America in 1798 in the form of roots, berries, and spices that she carried in this basket from her home in Scotland. Kathleen O'Brien had only one passion in life, and that was to save the lives of sick children. She planted in a small garden on the American soil her dream seeds of life for the future, and I stand here before you today as the fruit of her dream, the AWAKE medical breakthrough, which will give every child the opportunity to fulfill their own dream."

Annah listened intently as Kathleen recalled the stories of the lives of the women portrayed in the journals. It was when Kathleen came to the portion of the story surrounding the abortion clinic that Annah's palms moistened as she tightly held her journal.

"It was here in Ashton, Nebraska, that a woman who had been raped found herself on the steps of an alternative pregnancy center. But as this woman lay on the table just seconds before having an abortion, she realized something the women before her knew. She carried inside of her more than just an embryo; she carried within her a legacy passed down thru her generation. If she had undergone that abortion, I would not be standing before you today, and today we would not be celebrating a new medical breakthrough giving woman the one true alternative—to save the unborn child.

"In closing I want to thank some very special people. To my parents, who instilled in me a sense of destiny, who raised me to believe I was put on this earth to make a difference. Thank you. And to my biological mother, Dr. Savannah Grace Kentwell, who made the decision to give me life so our family's legacy would continue, thank you for choosing life."

As the audience applauded, Kathleen left the podium with the basket in her hand and walked down the aisle toward Annah. The audience continued its applause and cheering as Kathleen stood before Annah in tears.

"It is a pleasure to finally meet you, Dr. Savannah Grace Kentwell," Kathleen said.

"The feeling is mutual," Annah said, shaking her hand.

"I hope that we will have more opportunities to spend time together," said Kathleen.

"I would like that, too," Annah said as she smiled.

* * *

Annah repositioned her body to relax in the soft cushions of the rocking chair. From the porch of the two-story mansion, she could see mile after mile of green fields flirting with the sun setting over the Ashton horizon. She took several deep breaths, the fragrance vividly reminding her of the months she spent with Edward before he passed. She was delighted that she was still fully ambulatory minus her short-term memory. However, returning to Ashton encouraged her to reflect on how much she missed living there.

"Annah. Are you comfortable?" said Kathleen, adjusting the wrap on Annah's shoulders. "Is there anything I can get for you?"

"At ninety-three years old, I believe I have everything I need."

"Well, your grandchildren have finished their dinner, and if you are still up to it, I told them they could come out here on the porch and read to you."

"I wouldn't miss it for the world," Annah said.

In the background Annah could hear the children running through the house, and within seconds they burst through the front door, all six of them ages two through eight, each holding a book.

"Are you sure you are going to be okay here?" said Kathleen.

"I'll be just fine."

"Nana?" said Abigail, the youngest of Annah's grandchildren.

"Yes, Abigail."

"It's my turn to read you a story."

"I would love that, Abigail. And what shall I have the pleasure of hearing today?"

"Today, I want to read to you about airplanes." Abigail climbed up and nestled herself in Annah's lap. Annah smiled at her two-year-old granddaughter and listened as she read each word on the page.

"Abigail?" Annah said, interrupting her reading. "You are here to make a difference."

"I already know that, Nana," Abigail said in a matter-of-fact tone and continued reading with ease. Annah recalled that she had the same temperament when she was a small child. Annah sweetly kissed Abigail on the cheek. She was the only one among the six siblings who was a prodigy.

Kathleen watched Annah smiling, surrounded by her legacy, and with the sun setting Kathleen selected one of the journals from the sewing basket and opened to the first page.

"This journal belongs to Savannah Grace Kentwell and is dedicated to my daughter, Kathleen Clarice Whitman." Kathleen settled herself comfortably on the front porch swing, slowly turning the page as she began to read.

Choose life...

Choose life...

COMING SOON

The Promise

Constance Wright

Second book in the trilogy series